WHO DO YOU SAY THAT I AM?

Encounters with Jesus Based on the Gospels

CHERYL MADEWELL

WESTBOW
PRESS®
A DIVISION OF THOMAS NELSON
& ZONDERVAN

Unless otherwise indicated, all scripture quotations are from The Holy Bible,
English Standard Version (ESV). Copyright 2001 by Crossway Bibles, a division
of Good News Publishers. Used by permission. All rights reserved.
WestBow Press books may be ordered through booksellers or by contacting:

WestBow Press
A Division of Thomas Nelson & Zondervan
1663 Liberty Drive
Bloomington, IN 47403
www.westbowpress.com
1 (866) 928-1240

ISBN: 978-1-9736-0154-8 (sc)
ISBN: 978-1-9736-0155-5 (hc)
ISBN: 978-1-9736-0153-1 (e)

Library of Congress Control Number: 2017913772

Print information available on the last page.

WestBow Press rev. date: 10/13/2017

To Cookie's kids.

May you love Jesus and dream big all your lives. I love you all!

CONTENTS

ACKNOWLEDGMENTS

I am thankful for the Wednesday-afternoon SeniorLife ladies for listening to my story of the feeding of the five thousand and encouraging me to write more.

Thanks to Dr. Dennis Mock, Mel Sumrall, and Janis Saville for their vision for Bible Training Center for Pastors/Leaders. This program was instrumental for my training in Bible knowledge. Special thank-you to Janis for stretching me to be a storyteller.

A big thank-you goes to my "sisters" who encourage me and hold my feet to the fire when I need it. And an extra thanks to the Felicias; you know who you are. And to the rest of my church family at Denton Bible Church, your encouragement to grow, teach, and write is priceless.

For Nancy, Fran, Nan, Wileen, Kay, and Valda, who stepped in to love me like a mother would—encouraging, praying, and caring for me deeply. Each one of you has an amazing story of your encounters with Jesus.

I am thankful for growing up with friends with imaginations and not as much technology.

Most of all, I am thankful for Jesus, who saved me, gave me a creative mind, and put an everlasting yodel in my soul.

INTRODUCTION

As I grew up as an only child, my imagination was my best friend. Tea with the queen, not Kool-Aid and crackers; a servant cleaning a castle, not dusting my room; a pasture as my mansion, not a grazing field for the cows; solving mysteries like Nancy Drew; teaching school to my dolls; and dancing with kings on the back porch—these were the ways I spent my days. I was also a daydreamer. My mind would often take me on trips to far-off places, where I would meet the most interesting people. Flying off to Paris for fashion week; riding in the Rose Parade; traveling back in time to meet JFK, Coco Chanel, and so many more. By reading I became part of the story, and I wondered what the dishes the characters ate tasted like, what they were wearing, and about all the details of the story that were not on the page.

I asked why, how, where, who, what, and when about everything. I wanted to know the whole story.

When I became a Christian and started reading my Bible, I discovered many wonderful stories, but they were all too often just black and red letters on a page. I did not think there was room for my imagination in my walk with Christ. After all, the Bible is God's written word. Later, I attended the Bible Training Center for Leaders (BTCL) at Denton Bible Church. BTCL deepened my faith and gave me skills to teach the Bible to ladies. One of those skills was storytelling. I was intrigued by the accounts of the different teachers teaching to women around the world who could not read or who had no access to a Bible. For my final project for BTCL, I was asked to tell a story. I told the story of the feeding of the five thousand from a woman's perspective. None of the accounts of this story include this perspective. I looked at the culture and formed my story from what I knew and had learned. From that story on, I was taken back to my love of imagination as a child. With my imagination, the stories came to life. Jonah in the whale made me seasick; David's rock made a great thud in Goliath's forehead; I could smell the salty air as Israel crossed the Red Sea, and on and on. Every story I read came to life, no longer black text on the page but vivid colors, pungent smells, and exotic tastes. The Bible is a living Technicolor production. As I studied the Gospels, I wondered what it would have been like to walk with Jesus.

Enjoy these glimpses into the Gospels from someone who might have been there with Jesus.

CHAPTER 1

INSIDE THE TEMPLE WALLS

The Story of Anna

Love, total intimacy, ultimate delight, supreme fulfillment, unending respect, deep passion—this is how I describe my marriage. I was happy, happier and more joyous than I had even been the day I married my love, Elihu. Our love grew each day. He was the kind of husband who valued his wife. I was the ruby in his crown. Every day he would do something to show me how much he loved me and only me. He would bring me flowers, take me on long walks beside the stream, and spend hours with just me. My favorite times were when we would sing praises to the God of Abraham. Our voices blended in perfect harmony as they wafted toward the heavens. Elihu would keep the tempo by gently patting my thigh.

Elihu was from the tribe of Levi and served in the temple. He was a good man. He served the Lord with his whole strength. Every night he would come home, and we would talk way past twilight about

God, the prophets, and how to serve the God of Israel. My favorite stories were from the prophets—how the covenant between God and David would be fulfilled when the Messiah would come to rule over Israel. I prayed that the Messiah would come, and Elihu and I could serve Him together.

Then one horrible day, my love was taken from me. I awoke early, as I always did, and slipped quietly out of bed into the kitchen to begin to prepare breakfast. I opened the shutters to let in the pink light of sunrise as I set bread and fruit on the table. I quickly straightened my hair, pulling it back with my favorite blue scarf. Elihu said that the blue was a beautiful contrast to my raven-black hair. He was always commenting on my features. I thought I was plain looking, but to him, I was the most beautiful woman in the entire world. By now, he was usually up and ready to eat and say morning prayers with me before going to the temple gates to serve. I went back to the bedroom to see what was causing his delay. He was not awake, so I went to him to gently kiss him; he liked when I woke him this way. Sometimes he would pretend to be sleeping and, as I leaned in, would open his eyes and sit up. This always frightened me, and I would scream, and then we would both burst into laughter. I leaned in to kiss him, and he did not stir, he did not open his eyes, and he did not sit up. He was not breathing! I screamed and ran out to the street to find help.

"Help! Help! My husband is not breathing! Someone, please help me!"

Soon all our family and neighbors were there with me. I rushed back to the bedroom and began to shake him.

"Please breathe. Please wake up. Please!"

Seven years was not enough time. I felt as though I would stop breathing and wished that it would be so. I would join my love in Abraham's bosom. I did not know how I would survive without the perfect love we had experienced. My heart broke into a million pieces, and there was nothing that could heal it. I was twenty-four years old and a widow. What would my life become? He had brothers who could redeem me, but I refused. My broken heart could not love another man.

All our conversations about God and His prophets were the only bit of love and hope I had left. I would go where I could hear the priests and rabbis teach these things. After the year of long mourning, I moved to the temple to be a servant to the priests. And I would wait for the coming Messiah. Our King was coming. Elihu had said so, and I clung to every word and promise he had taught me from the scrolls.

Other women lived in the temple quarters with me as we served. We stayed in a house located inside the temple walls. Each room was modest and contained just enough for us to live comfortably. I shared my room with two other widows. Both of these older ladies had lost their husbands in the war against the Philistines, but because of the loss of men during the war, they had no kinsman redeemer. They had been in the temple for several years before I dedicated my life to service.

We rose early before the sun rose to wake the city, and our day began in prayer. I prayed for the Messiah to come. I knew that He could heal my heart. We would sweep the courtyard, prepare breakfast for the priests who lived within the walls like us, and tidy our chamber as the sun entered the new day. The city would wake to the soft, yellow light of the sun, and the bustling noise of commerce soon filled the air. Most days I chose to fast and pray for the soon-coming King. I would stay in the courtyard, pleading with God as people came in and out with sacrifices of all kinds. The priest would take the animals, grain, and oils into the inner courts and perform the rituals of sacrifice. When a burnt offering was sacrificed, sweet and savory aromas like the finest food would hang in the air. The fathers would speak with the priest and receive their family portion back— savory lamb, roasted bulls, and grains. The family would pause and eat the portion together before returning to their home. The festivals were busy times, and I could fade into the crowd and pray without interruptions. Other days I would minister to the ladies and children by offering them water and prayers.

As the sun was saying goodbye to the city, we would prepare food for the priests before retiring to our room. Once the sun had set, the noise of the day faded away, and I felt closer to God in my prayers. For sixty years, I have lived in the temple, and every day, I have remembered my husband and missed him. Sometimes I would see a man in the crowd who would make think that these sixty years were only a dream—he would look so much like Elihu. I would blink my old eyes and see that it was not him, and my body aches would remind me of my age.

Today began like every other day: doing my chores and praying. But as I prayed, I felt that I would soon see my King. The courtyard was not too busy, and I went to speak with a young lady holding her baby boy. He was not yet a month old, as they had come for the purification sacrifice. I felt drawn to this woman, and as I approached, I felt my heart leap. Surrounding her was an unusual yet familiar light and warmth—the feeling of hope. This precious baby boy was the Messiah. God had finally heard my prayers and let me see my King. Tears of sweet joy ran down my face. She let me hold Him! I rejoiced as I embraced my Lord! I spoke to Him as if He already knew me. In His eyes were kindness, love, and compassion deeper than I had ever experienced. The sparkle in His eyes made me feel more love than I had even felt with Elihu. I wanted to dance for joy and lift Jesus up into the air, but my old body would not let me. I would have held Him forever, but Mary needed to feed Him, and His eyes were tired from the long day. He smiled at me as I passed Him back to her. I went about the rest of my day with an extra charge of joy in my feeble steps.

As I drifted off to sleep that night, I thanked God again for answering my prayer. I asked Him to receive me now in death.

Based on Luke 2 English Standard Version.

CHAPTER 2

· ·

CANOPY OF COLORS

The Story of Jesus's First Miracle: Water to Wine

Every little girl in Canna pretended to be Rebekah as she dreamed of her wedding someday. One of us would be Abraham and send the pretend servant to find a bride for Isaac, his son. Abraham's most faithful servant went to Harran, the land where Abraham had sojourned years before. We would pack up the pretend camel and make our journey to the well. I hated being the camel, but we all took turns acting out each part. At the well of his master's fathers, the servant waited until a woman would come and offer to give him a drink. Of all the beautiful women who came to the well, the most beautiful drew water for him and for his camels. Rebekah was her name, and theirs was a romance we all loved.

Shiddukhin is the preliminary arrangement whereby the groom's father seeks out a wife for his son. This matchmaker's agreement could have been made when we girls were very little, even at our births.

The next step could have been years in the making. The arranging for the groom to support his wife-to-be and for the bride's family to list her dowry in writing were the first official steps in betrothal. There were many other legal steps to the beautiful day when the couple would meet under the huppah to become betrothed. Huppahs were made for each couple out of brilliantly colored linens. Sheer orange, brilliant blue, sparkling gold, and majestic purple drapes would blow in the wind off the ornately carved frame. Each was unique, with beads, needlework, and elaborate designs. Under the huppah, a ceremony was performed with wine and a promise of the groom not to let wine pass his lips until they were under the canopy again. At this point, although they were married, the couple parted ways for a year. Betrothal was a time for preparations for the couple's life together. The groom returned to his home and began to add on to his home a special room for the couple. This room had to meet the rabbi's approval when it was finished. The bride was supposed to be moving up in life, and the first symbol was her home. The bride had plenty to keep herself busy with too. As a bride myself, I knew how busy. I had several special wedding garments to sew. These weren't your normal sewing projects. There were specifications based on the law, plus I wanted to make sure I looked my most beautiful ever.

A year ago I was witness to my cousin Leah's betrothal. In Israel weddings involve your whole family. The whole village was there. Each family came together, young and old, to celebrate and witness the couple's joy. Over the last year, I visited her and saw the opulent gown and headdress she was making. We spoke with excitement, trepidation, and expectation of her groom coming. I told her stories of how my James had come for me and about the glorious day of our union and how kind and gentle he was. I assured her that what God ordains He blesses, and she was a blessed woman.

My James and I were happy to celebrate with my family as we waited for Leah's Andrew to come and take her to be his forever. The bride's family was not to know when the groom was to come claim his bride. We came to celebrate two weeks before the anniversary of their ceremony under the huppah. The men stayed mostly outside of the house while we waited. The ladies were inside tending to Leah's final preparations. There was her final cleansing, advice for the consummation, mud masks, and grinding of berries for face paint.

Her dress was scarlet, the color of a ripe pomegranate. To get such a bright color, she must have dyed the fabric several times. Her seams were straight, and the needlework was sheer perfection. When she first showed us, I could not help but squeal with delight.

Every night all of Canna would turn out to see if Andrew had come. We would feast, drink wine, and wait.

On the third day as the people were coming out, off in the distance there was something coming. Through the dust I could see some men dancing and waving banners. Then I heard the trumpets. He was coming! I spun around in excitement as I turned into the house wait with Leah for her Andrew. As we rushed to get her special dress on her, we all seemed to be dancing a jig. You could cut the excitement with a table knife. Several times I just laughed out loud for sheer joy of what was coming.

"He is here! He is here!" shouted the crowd. With all the ceremony befitting a queen, Leah's Andrew was there at the door. I was so joyful that I could not contain my giddiness or tears of joy.

Leah had been with me on my day, and now I was here celebrating hers. She was a lovely bride made lovelier by her heart of sweet devotion. The greatest feast was prepared, and we began to eat and drink. All of Canna was there, so I cannot imagine the amount of food or wine we consumed. Each day brought a new beautiful dress and matching headdress. She had worked so hard on each of these. Scarlet, magenta, chartreuse, sunshine yellow, and tangerine were the colors in which she wove her wardrobe. Each dress was more gorgeous than the one before.

Each dish of food was a work of art. The finest cooks and bakers had been hired. There were dolmas by the thousand, salty sardines baked with tahini that we scooped up with flat bread, endive and olives, roast duck and lamb, dates, almonds, pomegranates, grapes, apricots, and honey-dipped raisin cakes. You had to be careful with the raisin cakes because they were said to be an aphrodisiac, so we did not want anyone not married to eat one and be taken over by passion.

The men reclined at the main tables while the ladies had separate tables closer to the area where the food was kept. The food was in various baskets and jars and seemed to be limitless in supply. The wine was in large jars that held thirty gallons of wine. These were usually for collecting water from the spring rains.

The days began to run together, but I believe this happened on day three. Some men showed up and joined Mary, Joseph's wife. I had not seen him in a few years, but I believe it was her son, Jesus. I was not trying to eavesdrop, but I could not help but hear the oddest conversation. They did not talk softly, and I was there nibbling on some dates and almonds. Mary told Jesus there was no more wine. What did He have to do with wine making? Had He started a vineyard nearby? There would not be time to go anywhere and fetch more. What did she want Him to do?

His response was puzzling to me. He questioned her, as I would have. What did the lack of wine have to do with Him? He said, "Woman, what does this have to do with me? My hour has not yet come" (John 2:4 ESV). His hour? Was he supposed to bring the wine at a certain time?

All the sudden the music got louder, and a new group of dancers entered the courtyard. I got lost in their spins and the rhythm of the music. Jesus and Mary were no longer where my attention was. After the dancing was over, I looked back in the direction of where Jesus and Mary were talking. I did not hear their exchange, but she's a Jewish mother, so I would assume there was some guilt she placed on Jesus.

The most peculiar thing happened next. Mary instructed the wine servants to do whatever Jesus told them.

I thought He was going to instruct them to go somewhere and fetch more wine. But that was not at all what He did. He told them to fill the six jars with water. Once they were filled to the top, Jesus instructed the servant to draw out a glass and take it to the master of the banquet. Why would He send a cup of water to the master? Water was for cleaning and ceremonial cleansing, not for drinking at the banquet. As the servant passed by me I noticed this water was not clear, as it had gone into the jar. It was ruby red like the finest wine. I rubbed my eyes. What kind of trickery had Jesus and Mary pulled? I know what I saw. I just do not know how this water had turned to wine.

The banquet was abuzz over the new wine being brought out. This wine was the finest anyone had ever tasted. Even as I drank and tasted for myself, I did not know how this could be. Had Jesus turned this water to wine?

As I sat there pondering and sipping the sweetest wine I had ever tasted, I was once again lost in the music and dancers. I do not know how He did it, but Jesus had made the water into wine. When I went to lay with my husband that night, I told him all I had heard and seen. James just patted me on the head and said the heat and wine must have gone to my head. For the next three years, I would hear of more signs Jesus had done and wonder about that wedding day in Canna.

Based on the story of Jesus turning water to wine in John 2:1–12 ESV.

CHAPTER 3

TRADITION TURNS TO CHAOS

The Story of Jesus Cleansing the Temple

I did not expect the chaos I saw as the tables were turned over in sheer anger. Long gone were my simple childhood memories. My earliest memories were of traveling to Jerusalem with my family for Passover. My mother, aunts, and grandmother would pack a special dress for themselves and for all of us children. For the men, she packed their best tunics and most colorful mantels. Our family lived past Bethany, so we traveled for two days to get to Jerusalem. Our bedrolls of a linen blankets and woven straw mats would be tightly rolled and packed on the camels.

For weeks prior to Passover, the ladies consulted each other as to what food we would take—berries, cheese, dried fish, nuts, olives, bread, and wine in fresh wineskins would be placed in large baskets that hung off of the camel on each side. Each of us would carry a small wineskin of water. We would get a new wineskin each year, as the skin would stretch out and no longer hold liquid. We would fill these every day at the well near where we stopped. An ephod of fine flour would be carried separately for sacrifice, as would the olive oil. There would be a cage with two perfect turtledoves for each family. We would also take a lamb and young bull for the sacrifices.

All the families from my village also traveled to Jerusalem for the Passover. My brothers, sisters, and cousins played chasing games with the other travelers. The boys all knew each other from school at the local temple. We traveled at night and rested during the day. We had heard of many people being robbed when they traveled by sunlight. My father had learned from his father how to navigate by using the stars. Sometimes my brothers would walk with Father and ask questions about the constellations. They would all bring their families to Jerusalem. Each of the men carried a heavy walking stick. Grandfather's was the most ornate. Carved from acacia wood, at the top there was a claw holding on to a sphere. The length was olive branches and grapevines intertwined, and the wood was darkened at the spot where he gripped the stick. I believed he could have fought off any bear, mountain lion, or robber we encountered. However, he never had to on our trips.

> On the last day of our journey, we would sing as we
> entered Jerusalem,
> I lift up my eyes to the hills.
> From where does my help come?

My help comes from the Lord,

who made heaven and earth.

He will not let your foot be moved;

he who keeps you will not slumber.

Behold, he who keeps Israel

will neither slumber nor sleep.

The Lord is your keeper;

the Lord is your shade on your right hand.

The sun shall not strike you by day,

nor the moon by night.

The Lord will keep you from all evil;

he will keep your life.

The Lord will keep

your going out and your coming in

from this time forth and forevermore.

(Psalm 121 ESV)

Once we were inside the city gate, my uncles would arrange for a tent for our stay. There were other relatives who lived inside the city gates where we would have our Passover meal. After getting us settled into our temporary home, the women would hurry to my aunt's mother-in-law's house to make the Passover preparations. My older cousins were left to look after us. We would sit at the tent door and watch the other families coming into town. I would make up imaginary stories of their lives and tell stories to the others. The city was charged with energy that you could feel. From our door I could see the market. There were booths as far as the eye could see selling the choicest fruits, vegetables, and nuts. The figs were an amazing color of deep purple, along with bright red pomegranates and sharp green olives. The ladies selling scarves and fabrics were my favorite to look at—red fabric with golden camels woven in sheer, brilliant blues, and regal purples blew in the wind, making waves of rainbow colors. Tomorrow we would go to the temple and make our sacrifices but today, I would sit and take in all that was happening.

Women and children and even boys until the age of thirteen were not allowed into the temple's inner courts. At Passover each year I went into the Court of Women and Gentiles to worship and pray. Singing joyous songs and dancing praises to the God of Abraham were such a delight. My mother would hold on to our hands as we entered with thousands of other worshipers. People would be pushing to stay with their families. The men would go deeper into the temple to make sacrifices. I had seen the high priest go past us one day. His robe was brilliant purple with stones representing each tribe sparkling at his neck. The bells that were sewn into the hem fascinated me. I learned that these were so the other priests could tell if he was still moving in the Holy of Holies. A cord was tied around his leg that ran out into the outer court so he could be pulled out if God took him because of his sins.

As When I was a woman, my husband brought us to Jerusalem, and I prepared my family. Today the temple court looked more like a market than the actual market. There was a buzz all over Jerusalem; gone were the days of bringing your own sacrifice to the temple. If you had money, any man could purchase sheep, goats, doves, pigeons, and grains inside the temple walls. Moneychangers and these sellers of sacrifice set up tables and tents. This was not troublesome to the Pharisees, so buying a sacrifice must have been permitted. Being a woman, I did not know all the laws like my husband and brothers.

As we entered Jerusalem, we went straight to the temple to make annual atonement for our sins. We brought a perfect lamb, two turtledoves, grain, and oil to give the priest as sacrifice for our sins. I tightly gripped my children's hands as we set foot inside the outer court for the women and Gentiles. Gone were my childhood romantic visions of the court. An uneasy feeling swept through my body as we passed each stall of moneychangers and sellers of sacrifice.

Suddenly I saw Him. He was angry. He began turning over the tables and driving out the evildoers. Livestock scurried in every direction, trampling over anything in its way. I scooped up my youngest daughter as a bull charged past us. Feathers floated through the air as all the birds began to fly away. He made a whip of cords and drove all the men out of the temple. There were coins flying through the air and making clanging noises as they hit the stones in the courtyard. My children clung to me tighter, and I tried to soothe them with hushed whispers so as not to draw attention to us. In the chaos I had lost my direction and did not know which way to move to my family out of this crazy place. Dust, feathers, and fear froze my movements. My husband spoke my name and led us out into the street with all those trying to get out of the way of the oxen, bulls, and sheep that were charging in all directions.

We slipped down an alley and found an open doorway in which to take refuge. We stood there for what seemed like an eternity. I breathed deeply and calmed down before we went to our borrowed tent for the night. I asked my husband if he knew the man who had turned over the tables and caused the chaos. He said he heard His name was Jesus. That was the only day I saw Jesus, but I heard all about His wonderful miracles for the next three years.

Based on John 2:13–22 and Psalm 121 ESV.

CHAPTER 4

THE SUN FROM MY WINDOW

The Story of Nicodemus

The sky was striped with majestic purple and brilliant orange as the large yellow sun sank behind the dark mountains surrounding Jerusalem. I had heard stories of earlier that day when a rabbi named Jesus had caused a great commotion when He overturned the tables and stalls in the temple. My husband was a Pharisee, and he had come home with a heavy heart. To lead the Jews in this time was difficult. There were some who wanted to kill Jesus and others who were following Him. My husband was conflicted because he had heard of all the amazing signs Jesus was performing, but many of his close friends and colleagues were plotting to kill Him because of the rumors that He was going to overthrow Pilate and make Himself king. When I went to the well and the market, I heard many rumors about Him too. For many nights we had lain awake talking about what we had seen and heard about Jesus.

The indigo sky was dotted with flickers of yellow from lamps and candles lit for the evening. Soon the city would fade into a blanket of black sky and distant stars. It would be quiet then. My husband had found out where Jesus was staying and planned to slip off in the deep dark of the night to go and meet Him. He kissed me goodbye to ease my worries and fears. What if he was caught? What would the other Pharisees do to him? My husband was a well-respected leader in the temple—he was not one to stir up trouble. He was a rule and tradition follower. But tonight he had to seek Him. Out into the cold night air my husband slipped quietly with no lantern, just the stars to guide his steps. He moved with a fast caution—careful to place his foot softly on solid stones in the road.

He found the house where Jesus was and found Him quickly. My husband and Jesus talked most of the night—I paced the floor worrying about if he had found the rabbi or was caught by others. I wanted to hear all the things my husband had found out about Jesus. Was he really to be king? Had those people been healed, or had it been a trick? Soon my husband would have to be home—the sky was changing from indigo to navy, and the sun would soon bring forth yellow and orange rays of warmth.

Hurry! I thought as I circled the room again. Then the door swung open. Nicodemus was home. I ran to him and embraced him. I began to weep for joy. My husband was home. He held me tight while the tears flowed from my tired eyes. Then he raised my chin with his finger so that I was looking in his eyes. There was something different in his eyes. He kissed me gently and asked me to sit with him while he told me all that had happened that night.

I warmed some water for tea as we sat by the fire. He first told me that he believed that no one had seen him as he quickly went through the streets. Jesus was still awake when he reached the house, almost as if He were waiting to meet with him. Nicodemus had started the conversation by telling Jesus that he believed He was from God because of the signs and wonders He manifested. Jesus then began to tell Nicodemus how to become a true follower of Him, which was by rebirth. I was confused by this "rebirth." My husband said that he too was perplexed by this term and asked how a grown man could go back to the womb. All I could imagine was the birth of my children, and I could not even begin to think about putting them back inside my womb. Nicodemus must have seen my utter terror at this thought and pulled me closer to him and told me that there were two types of birth—of a woman and of the Spirit. I encouraged him to tell me more, as my mind was calm again. I nestled my head against his chest in order to hear his heart beat while he shared about the Spirit. With each deep breath, he spoke about how kind Jesus had been when telling him about being born again. I felt Nicodemus shudder and his voice crack as he told me about how God had loved each of us in the world and how God sent His only son. We had one son, and I could not imagine our lives without him. But God sent Jesus to show His love for us and to save us from sins. I told Nicodemus that I thought the priest was the one to make our sacrifices—that he was the one to represent our family to God. He pulled me closer and ran his hands down my hair as he hugged me tightly and said that Jesus would be better than a priest or Pharisee. Better than my Nicodemus? I could not think of anyone better. He then told me that he had been born again that night and I could be born again too. He explained that I needed to just trust that Jesus is the Son of God and begin to follow His teaching.

I lifted my head to look at him square in the face. There in his eyes was a light—a dancing sparkle that was not there before. His face seemed to be glowing and where I had seen worry, I saw joy. Nicodemus said that following Jesus would bring persecutions and would be hard. We might lose everything because he could no longer be a Pharisee. Our eyes locked, and I said I would go wherever he was going. We clasped hands and rejoiced together as we prepared for the new adventure. We opened the curtains and looked east for the new day's sun. The sun was lighting the mountains, and the sky was brilliant blue with rays of vivid yellow, striking orange, and welcoming pink. We stood at the window with his arms wrapped around me, both lost in our own thoughts of this new life. I felt warm, secure, and protected. I trusted my husband, and that night I trusted in Jesus.

Our lives were forever changed …

Based on the story of Nicodemus as told by John in chapter 3 ESV.

CHAPTER 5

....

SPIT ON THE GROUND

The Story of the Blind Man

I am an observer—looking at the world around me to see all the details: drops of dew on a blade of grass, the chaff as it blows through the air on winnowing day, the vivid colors of the scarves in the market, the red of a pomegranate, the blue of the sky, and the white of the clouds. The world is full of color. I cannot imagine not seeing these colors and shapes. Growing up, there was a boy who lived next door. He was born blind. I felt sorry for him when the other children and I would play. He would sit by the road and beg. Every day he was in total blackness, void of even a sparkle of light—the sadness of nothingness.

His life was reduced to begging. The other children were so cruel. They would move things into his path so he would trip, or they would just push him over. He was covered in scrapes and bruises from the falls. Some would go over to him and wave their arms, and when he failed to wave back, they would hit him in the face. He did not get to go to temple and learn like my brothers and the other boys. He was not promised in marriage. He could do no job, and all he could do was beg. Every day his father or mother would lead him to the main gate, where he would sit and beg all day. Some days he received a few coins, but all too often his cup was left empty. I think his life must have been like his cup—empty. At home he used a walking stick to find his way, and their house and yard were laid out in a specific pattern that was easy for him to remember.

I overheard the adults talk about him many times wondering; had *he sinned or his parents* (John 9:3 ESV)? His family was very similar to mine, so I could not think of anything they had done to make him blind. I was not an adult, but I wondered about him too. I wondered what darkness was like. Was it like a rainy night with no stars? Was it dark like the bottom of Jacob's well? Was there no light like the inside of a tomb? I wanted to know how he knew it was I when I gave him bread or a cool drink of water. I wondered if he was afraid that his parents might die and leave him alone. But most of all, I wondered if God knew he had done this to my friend. Why had God been so cruel? Blindness is the worst punishment.

In the last few days, I had heard of a man teaching about God. He taught about the goodness of God and His great mercy. I wanted to tell this man that he was wrong. A God who makes people blind is not good at all! I tried to get close to the man, but there were thousands of people trying to get close to Him to be healed. I heard of His healing powers. He had walked past my friend coming into the city, and He did nothing. I was upset—sad, angry, then sad all over again. Why was my friend overlooked to be healed? I struggled to go to temple. I did not want to worship a God who did not care for my friend. I began to make excuses not to go worship with my family. This Sabbath I said that I felt queasy and needed to rest. As soon as I knew my family had gone, I got up, stretched, and went for a walk. I made sure to stay in the boundaries of not working on the Sabbath by only walking a short distance, just enough to clear my head and be home before my family.

As I turned to enter our gate, I heard a familiar voice behind me, calling my name. I whirled around thinking I had been caught by my family only to see my friend. He was alone with no walking stick, so I rushed to him, thinking he needed my help. There was something different about him—his eyes were no longer murky white. They were brown, clear, with a sparkle of joy in them. He began to recount his day minute by minute. After breakfast he had gone to take his place by the temple gate with help from his father. As he sat there begging, the teacher came up and began talking to him. Suddenly he heard the man spit, and then there was a mud on his face. He thought at first that this was some joke spitting in the mud and rubbing on the blind man's eyes. But as the teacher spoke to him, he realized that the teacher was sincere. He was instructed to go wash in the pool of Siloam.

Someone took him by the arm and led him to the pool, where he washed the mud and spit off of his eyes. He told me that the light hurt his eyes at first, but soon he was seeing all the wonderful things I had explained to him as a child. He gathered his robes and ran as fast as he could back to the place where the teacher had been. The teacher had slipped into the crowd. There were several Pharisees in the crowd that day and they began to question my friend. *"One thing I do know, that though I was blind, now I see"* (John 9:25 ESV) was all my friend could say. He did not know how he had been granted sight or who had preformed this great miracle. As we were rejoicing together, the crowd moved from the temple to outside of our houses.

A group of Pharisees pushed past us to his gate and began demanding to know what happened from his parents. His mother was shaking as her husband answered that my friend could answer for himself. A group of Jewish leaders was there too. They accused his parents of pretending their son was blind. I wanted to scream, "No one would pretend to be blind! It is a horrible life!" But as they pointed in our direction, I began to be fearful for my friend. Was washing the mud off considered work? Would they drag him back to the market to stone him?

The Pharisees angrily hurled questions at him.

"Are not you the blind man?"

"Where is the man that healed you?"

"Do not you know you cannot work on the Sabbath?"

"How did He open your eyes?"

"What was it that He put on your eyes?"

"Do not you know this man is a sinner?"

"How can a sinner do such amazing signs?"

"What do you say about Him since He has opened your eyes?"

As I stood there trembling in fear, one of them pointed at me. "Is this the man born blind?" he shouted.

I shook my head in agreement as I tried to press into the crowd to become invisible. My friend moved in front of me and with all the boldness I have ever seen said, *"I have told you already, and you would not listen. Why do you want to hear it again? Do you also want to become his disciples?* (John 9:27 ESV) Will you join me in searching for him?"

As those words hung in the air the Pharisees and Jews began to spit on the ground and began spewing insults. "Sinner! Blasphemer! You have done trickery from Beelzebub."

All the men who had come to accuse my friend slipped away one by one. My friend would not back down. He stood firm against the entire crowd. Soon we were standing alone with Jesus. He had returned to the market as the Pharisees left because He heard that the Jews had cast him out. My friend knew the voice of Jesus although he had never seen His face. Jesus had a soothing voice that made me feel peaceful and calm. All my fears drifted away. As they talked, my friend and I saw Jesus for who He was. He was the Son of God. I knew for sure what He said was true, for I had seen the miracle of sight in my friend. Once he was blind, but now he sees.

I see things a little differently now too. My eyes were open as well, and I saw God glorified in the giving of sight. He was not a mean, judgmental God like that of whom the Pharisees teach. He is kind and gentle and sent His Son for my friend. And for me!

Based on the story of the blind man in John 9 ESV.

CHAPTER 6

. . . .

OVERFLOWING BASKETS

The Story of the Feeding of Five Thousand

I was in the middle of doing my daily chores—washing the clothes, folding up the linens, rolling up the sleeping mats, milking the goat, preparing meals for the day, gathering firewood, and fetching water. As I was kneading the bread for the day, my husband came running and shouting.

"Come quickly! Come *now!*"

Was someone hurt? Had the ox cart fallen over—perhaps on one of the children? I followed my husband down the rocky path to the main trade road. I felt every stone on the path through my thin leather sandals as I ran frantically looking for my little ones! Near the main road I spotted them, counting … one, two, three, four, five! All there! The ox cart was upright. What was causing my husband's excitement?

My husband, Eli, is a hard worker, provides for us, and

faithfully goes to the temple at all the appointed times. He is steady-as-you-go and not easily excited, so you can imagine my curiosity when he came home running and shouting! I knew this had to be colossal, and I had to see for myself what the excitement was all about.

As we ran unto the main road leading to the sea, now with kids in tow, Eli began to explain. It seemed there was a man named Jesus who was doing miracles in our region. He had healed an official's son. The official was from Cana and had heard of Jesus's miracles. The official asked Jesus to come to his home to heal the boy, but Jesus did not go to the man's home and lay His hands on the boy like the pagan priests who chanted and danced around burring pots of incense. Jesus said because of the official's faith in the power and deity of Jesus, his son would be healed by the time he returned home.

Have you ever heard of such a thing? He did not go with the official; Jesus just spoke the words and the boy was completely healed. It was like the boy had never been sick. I had heard about this man, Jesus, but I had my doubts. I had never seen one man with such power. Could His acts be real, or was He doing tricks of some kind?

Suddenly my family was in an overwhelming crowd of people. Even on a road wide enough for four ox carts to travel side-by-side, we were no longer able to run because of the sheer number of people. You could not stop to catch your breath for fear of being knocked over or climbed over. Everyone was pushing to get close enough to hear Jesus or maybe touch Him.

It was at that moment I was painfully aware of how disheveled I was. I remembered I was covered in flour. In my hurry I had not even taken off my apron. What would other ladies think of me?

I also realized it was getting close to our noon meal. If we did not turn around now, we would not get home in time to eat. Eat? What would we have to eat? I had not finished making the bread, and the stew was surely burned and ruined by now. My favorite pot would be damaged, my husband and children would go hungry, and my reputation would be of this disheveled, crazy woman who did not care for her own family. As I fretted, tears began to run down my cheeks, creating paths though the road dust and flour.

But all the ladies in the crowd were completely unaware of my unsightly appearance and me—they all had their eyes on Jesus and were pressing to get close to him.

I heard people around me talking about turning water into wine, healing the blind, lame, and leprous, and other miracles this Jesus had preformed. My mind was filled up with concerns for goats, pots, stew, bread, and hunger. My worries were dizzying, or maybe it was my growing hunger.

Then in the distance I saw Him! His appearance was nothing special to look at, but there was something about Him I could not quite grasp—perhaps it was His countenance or the tone of His voice— there was something that is so warm, inviting, peaceful, and perfect about His presence. I do not know how, but He saw me too! In that entire crowd of thousands upon thousands, He looked at me. It was not in the way other men look at women. Rather, He seemed to look deep into my soul. I cannot explain it, but in that moment, I felt the most complete love I ever experienced. It felt like the sunshine on the first day of spring that warms your body head to toe.

The thousands of other families, people who had followed Jesus to the grassy hill beside the sea, surrounded my family. I had never seen this many people here on this hill though I had been here often on my way from trading my vegetables and creamy goat cheese with fishermen for fish. It was a long walk to the seaside, but I enjoyed it and so did my children. They would run barefoot through the soft grass on the rolling hillside, and I would sit and talk with my friends while enjoying the salty breeze from the sea. I had not noticed how far we had walked until I felt the familiar breeze; we had gone through town and almost to the sea. Jesus instructed the crowd to sit down while His followers used their hands to make motions that we were to sit in small groups. My family joined another family from our village and sat down. Thousands of us were sitting on the side of the hill. There were families from the villages, and there were families from the city; it looked like everyone in the whole region had followed Jesus and his disciples this day.

I settled in with my family, straining to hear what He was going to say. I had forgotten about my hunger as I watched Him speak to His followers. All the teachers had men who followed with them. One of my sons asked what I had brought for them to eat for lunch. At that moment, my worries and hunger flooded back. I looked away from my son toward Jesus out of desperation for a solution for our hunger, and I did not want my son to see my new tears. I saw one of His followers bring a boy to Him. The boy handed Him something. It looked like the lunch sack I sent with my kids when they worked in the field. My children's lunch sack was made of goat hide and tied with straw; I would give them five small pieces of bread and two cured grey mullets. Grey mullets swim very close to the shore; sometimes I let the kids take baskets to the shore by this grassy hill to catch these fish. They made a game of who could get the most in the basket with one dip in the sea waves. They thought it was fun, and it provided fish I did not have to trade for, which was a blessing. The small lunch was enough to fill the stomachs of my children. I would pack three times as much for my husband. Jesus was leaning in and talking to the boy.

Jesus began to pray aloud; the crowd grew silent. All of us were focused on Jesus and His disciples, waiting to see what He was going to do next. Surely He was not going to eat the child's lunch in front of this hungry crowd. As I watched, I saw the disciples come to Him and begin to pass large straw baskets among the crowd. The baskets were like the fishing baskets—sturdy, loosely woven so that water could escape as you fished. We were some of the last to follow Him that day, so we were near the back of the crowd. I wondered if He intended for us all to fish for our own lunch there in the nearby sea. The followers delivered a large basket to each group. As soon as their arms were empty they returned to Jesus, and He gave them more baskets. There were thousands of baskets. Where had these all come from? when the boy was with Him, all I saw was the tiny lunch sack. As the baskets got closer to my family, I saw they were filled with bread and fish. Where did all this food come from?

The bread I took from the basket was the best I had ever eaten. Who made all this bread? Who caught all these fish? We weren't near a town where the food might have been purchased. The people were all focused on Jesus's teaching and waiting expectantly for His next miracle; no one had left to go fishing.

His followers invited us to eat as much as we wanted. We ate until we were all full, yet there were still fish and bread remaining in the basket. I offered our basket to another group, but each group had leftovers in their own baskets. When everyone on the hillside had eaten their fill, all the baskets were passed forward. There were twelve overflowing baskets filled with bread and fish. This was indeed miraculous! Jesus had fed thousands of people abundantly on only five loaves and two fish! A child's portion had fed everyone as far as the eye could see!

Jesus spoke for a while, and then we all slowly returned to our homes. No one wanted to leave; we were hanging onto every word He spoke, but He asked us to return to our homes and tell others of what we had seen and heard.

As we made our way home, we talked about this amazing man, His miracles, and the words He spoke to the crowd that day. We were convinced that this man Jesus was the promised, long-awaited Prophet, the Messiah!

As we approached our home, I saw my goat tied up. My fire had gone out so my pot was not ruined and my stew was not burned. I? Well, I was rejoicing, for I had seen Jesus!

We planned to get up early and return to the grassy hill where

He had been. But the next morning, a passer-by told my family that Jesus had crossed the sea, but in a most unusual way. But that's another story for another day.

Based on John's account of the feeding of the five thousand in John 6:1– 14 ESV.

CHAPTER 7

. . . .

WATER PITCHERS

The Story of the Samaritan Woman

Stifling heat! Hot! Dusty! Dirty! This was every midday. No proper lady would be working now; we were in our homes and tents resting after a noontime meal. Men, also, stopped in the middle of the day to rest at home or under large shade trees in the fields. The streets would be clear from all people except for *her*. She was no lady. Yes, she was a female, but after her five husbands, what man would want her? Her family had died when she was young, and so she sought a husband to care for her. The first was an older man whose wife had died in childbirth; he wanted a slave to cook, clean, and take care of his children and his needs. He died suddenly in his sleep, and his first son took his house and all the possessions but not her.

She was again in the streets looking for a way to provide for her needs. Women do not have the same benefits of a man; she had very few options—slave, harlot, beggar, or wife. Husbands two, three, and four treated her like a harlot and tossed her out to move on to younger women. I believe that number five truly loved her and wanted to take care of her. When he died, they were childless and his brother who had not approved of her the whole time would not redeem her and turned her out into the street again.

Now she lived with another man—she was not married to him, and he used her for profit as a harlot. As a young woman she had been beautiful, the kind of beauty that will turn a man's head—thick jet black hair that cascaded down her back, ruby red lips outlined her sparkling smile, high cheekbones, and eyes clear, the color of ripe dates. Desperation and harsh treatment had taken its toll on her physically, and she no longer walked with her head held high; her hair was thinning and left bald spots, her lips were faded and chapped, gone was her smile, her face sunken from lack of meals, and her eyes were blood shot from crying and lack of sleep. I did not know if I should pity her or hate her for what she did.

I imagine that if her first husband would have lived longer, we might have been friends—talking each morning at the well where we drew our water, cooking meals together while our kids played in the yard around us, or worshiping God together when we went to Mount Gerizim. I could not befriend her now because I would be a scandalous woman too.

Every day I knew she would walk past my house to the Well of Jacob to draw water in the middle of the day. She would do this quickly and return to her man. Today I did not notice her walking back as she had every day.

"Come, see a man who told me all that I ever did. Can this be the Christ?" (John 4:29 ESV).

"Come and see! Come and drink the Living Water," she shouted as she ran frantically past my home to the town square. I thought, *She has gone mad. Her horrid life has finally driven her mad.*

A man at the well? Hmmm! That would never happen; drawing water was woman's work. She must be seeing things.

She kept yelling and shouting over and over about a man who knew everything about her and living water. Slowly the people began to edge out of their houses. Out of curiosity, we all wanted to see what if anything was there. Her man led the way, with the leaders of the village following close behind. In the distance through the waves of heat I saw a man sitting on the ledge of the well. I rubbed my eyes, making sure I was not seeing a mirage. He was real, but was He mad too?

There was a man there, and it would be no surprise for him to know everything about her. All the Samaritans knew everything about her. She must know that her scandalous life made for the tastiest gossip. I had never seen this man before. He was not from our village. Had her life become the gossip of the whole region? The closer I got, I could see that this man was not Samaritan. I gasped out loud; He was a Jew. What would this Jew be doing here? They wanted nothing to do with us. We were mortal enemies. We did not walk through their cities, and they did not come through ours. This man must be mad. As my head was swimming with thoughts of what this madman might do to us, a group of men walked up and offered Him food. He waved His hands as if to say no, and the men sat nearby and began to eat. He stood up and began to talk to the crowd in a steady, calming cadence. The crowd was soon silent, leaning in to hear every word He spoke. We had never seen a Jew take an interest in us as He did.

He looked into our eyes as He spoke of divine love, forgiveness of sins, and Living Water. He walked through the crowd, speaking to each of us individually. My heart raced as He approached me. I had seen Him lean in, whispering in hushed tones to those before me. Some had tears of sorrow and joy as He spoke to them. What was He saying? Was He telling them of their past like He had the harlot earlier that day?

He came near me and leaned in and whispered, "Your sins are many, but today, you are forgiven because of your trust in me." As the thoughts formed in my mind—who was this man to forgive sins? He answered in a voice of absolute power, "I am Jesus, The Christ."

As He moved away from me, He began to speak of the prophecies He had fulfilled. I knew my faith had made me whole. I was forgiven. I wanted to fall down at His feet and worship right there in the dust by the well, but my pride stopped me. Examining the crowd, I searched for eyes that looked like they had heard His message of forgiveness too. The crowd thinned out; the majority left the well, spitting on the ground and muttering curses upon the Jews. Only those who wanted to trust in Jesus remained. He taught us many things about faith and our Father, God in heaven. As Jesus left the well to continue

His journey, I wondered how my life would be different. Drawing water would always remind me of that day, of that man, of Living Water, of Jesus.

Based on the woman at the well told by John in chapter 4 ESV.

CHAPTER 8

MAN-SIZED HOLE

Peter's Mother-in-Law's Story

I was a healthy woman, but as I aged, my feet did not move as fast, my arms grew weary when rocking a baby, and my back ached as I carried the water jar. All my friends felt the same, so I knew this was simply old age. My husband died, leaving me a widow. Life for a widow is hard, especially with no sons. My daughter and her husband moved in with me to help care for me as I aged. She and Peter were a delight to have in my home.

Peter had spent less time at home for the past few months, for he was following a new rabbi named, Jesus. There was something special about Jesus. He performed outlandish miracles that could have only come directly from God. Peter had brought Jesus and the other followers to my home several times. We would eat together, and Jesus would tell us amazing stories about heaven and the God of Abraham. His followers would relate the tales of His latest miracles—lame men walking, demons driven out, the blind seeing, water turned into wine, and lepers without blemish. Jesus and His men called my house home when in Capernaum.

On this on special day, my daughter sent word to Peter that I had taken ill and was about to die. I had a very high fever, shaking and seeing things that were not there. My body was exhausted. I was resigned to the fact that my time had come. Soon I would be dead. My daughters would prepare my body with linen strips soaked in nard and other spices, and then I would be placed in the tomb beside my sweet husband. I had prepared his body, my tears mixed with the spices as I placed each linen strip into place. All of my family came to mourn with me. They would be coming back to weep and mourn with my daughters. Soon I felt my life slipping away. It was hard to breathe. What was real? I was ready to be welcomed into Abraham's bosom. One last labored breath ...

Suddenly I felt warm and tingly all over. Was this the feeling of death? The warmth was rising up from my hand. Someone was holding my hand. As I opened my eyes, I expected to see the angelic being that had brought me to heaven, but I saw Jesus. Suddenly I felt amazing! I had no fever; no pain in my back, no chills. The world was in focus. I was healed! The warmth from my hand was the healing power of Jesus. Jesus had healed me!

Surrounding me was a multitude of people. People had followed Jesus to my house. My house! I quickly arose and began to serve. I straightened the bedcovers where I had been lying and went into the main room. The women in the room looked up from their weeping and squealed with amazed delight. We praised God, clasped hands, and danced about, showing our utter joy to God on High. I had been healed! We needed a banquet to celebrate. My daughters rejoiced with me and then began to make preparations for all these people. We made bread and put on pots of lamb stew. More water must be fetched. Wine had to be put into pitchers, grapes and pomegranates needed to go on platters, and nuts had to be brought from my food storage. People in the town had come to my house for mourning, but now there was great rejoicing. I was healed! Healed! Even I could not believe that I was healed. Jesus was the Promised Messiah. When He touched me, I felt the power of God rush through me. All I had, all I could do must be for Jesus. I could never repay all He had done for me that day.

I quickly went to tie back the curtains that had been drawn in my illness. Light—the house needed to be filled with light. As I flung open the front door to invite Peter and the other disciples in to join the banquet, I saw hundreds of people coming to my house. I stepped out into the crowd to welcome these people to my home. I had never seen so many people; they were all asking me about being healed. I retold the story as I went through the crowd hugging the people and weeping tears of joy with them.

The disciples found a place for Jesus to recline while those who needed His amazing healing came to Him one by one. Some were afflicted from birth with lame legs, blindness, and deafness; others had injured their backs. Legs and arms had been broken; some suffered with bleeding. All needed a simple word from Jesus, and they were whole. Praising and rejoicing of great magnitude followed each one's experience with Jesus. We were all healed!

I had seen those possessed by demons in the distance at the tombs where they kept some of them chained up but never in my own house. He was covered in sores, oozing scabs, dirt, and his own waste. Four men struggled to keep him contained. As he approached Jesus, he was struggling to be free from their grip, from the judging eyes he had long seen, from the demons inside him. As he fought, he growled, yelled words I had never heard, and bit at the air of his invisible oppressors. A cold wave of utter fear rushed through my body. Jesus stood as they approached, held out His hand, and with one simple word—away— the demons were gone. He was no longer cursing, growling, and biting. I offered him clean clothes and a basin to wash. Soon he was rejoicing and praising God with all of us who were healed.

I do not know how many people were healed along with me that night, for Jesus healed all who came. We had to light the torches and lanterns in the courtyard. They came way into the night for a special touch from my Lord, Jesus the Christ.

Before the light of dawn, I crawled into my bed thinking of all those healed and how hours earlier I had laid here ready for my death. Now I could dream of my future serving Jesus.

As the rooster crowed, I stretched, remembering all that had happened the night before. I pulled my hair up and put on my dress and apron. Breakfast needed to be made, water fetched, and I was sure there would be some cleanup from all the people last night. Once in the main room, I saw the people had not left as I assumed they would.

I had to be careful not to step on the ones who had made my floor their bed. Jesus was still reclining in my house, and they were still bringing all these people to Him. Jesus looked tired. Why did not He turn them away so He could rest? I wanted time to talk to Him alone, but that was not going to happen today. There was a line wrapped around my house of all these sick people.

I found a scrap of bread on the table and quickly gobbled it up for fear I would find no other food in my home. I felt my home groaning as more and more people forced their way into the main room. They were pushing and shoving to get close to my Jesus. People were in every corner of my house, sitting on the cushions, on the floor, hanging from the rafters, straining in the windows. I thought there were more people there than lived in all of Israel.

Could not Jesus just send them away? Maybe walk with them down by the sea? The grassy hillside by the sea would be a great place for all these sick, dirty people. He could teach them, and they would be able to move about more freely. My house could not fit one more person. I could not move anymore. The people kept coming. I found a corner and hoped this was all a nightmare. Suddenly dust fell on my head. I looked up to see what was causing the dust and noises. A hole in my ceiling! Men were lowering another man through my ceiling! They had no right! Where did they think this man was to be placed? There was not a single inch of room in my house.

Could not Jesus see that after all these people left, my house would be left in shambles? He and His disciples would move on to spread the Good News, and I would be the one left to put my house back in order. An old woman has no business being on top of a roof fixing a man-sized hole. I would fall and break my neck. I thought serving Jesus was going to be delightful, but not today. Today serving felt like a nightmare.

There were so many prostitutes and unclean people in my house. I loved Jesus, but I did not know that serving Him meant all the people. These people were no respecters of time. If Jesus was in my home— the people were coming to Him; He made my home His for the last three years of His life. He was so gracious, but some days I just could not take all the people. And the Pharisees—they were always lurking around. They came to try to find reasons to accuse Jesus. The sinners came seeking forgiveness and healing.

The twelve repaired the roof before they set off for their next journey with Jesus. There were always a few of the followers who stayed back to rest; they were helpful, and my house was soon in order. God had always smiled down on me and provided all that I needed—it was just hard to see with men coming through my roof. Many more days Jesus would come home. And try as we might, I do not think He ever got to rest fully. I was blessed, and I pray that I was a blessing to my Jesus. He was my Healer! He was my Lord! He filled my poor widow's heart with extreme joy!

Based on Matthew 8 ESV.

CHAPTER 9

. . . .

THE STORY WAS REAL

The Story of the Prodigal Son

A large crowd had gathered outside of the temple. I had walked to the market to sell my master's wool. I stopped as I heard the man telling stories. He had a voice that was so peaceful and passionate at the same time. I found a place in the shade and sat to listen. I had to; He had drawn me in with His words. I listened to Him tell about the lost sheep, the lost coin, and the lost son. As He told about the lost son. I recalled my master and his lost son.

Faithfully around the ninth hour, my master would go up onto the hill that looks toward the city. There he would talk to the God of Jacob, watch, and wait for his beloved son to return home. None of us thought his ungrateful son would return home. He had demanded his father give him his share of the inheritance. My master was so gracious that he gave the demanding younger son what was due to him upon his father's death. This son was greedy with his eyes on the world; his demands were a slap to his father as he had basically said he did not care if his father lived or died. My master was overcome with sadness, but he loved the son and did not want to withhold any blessing. Tears ran down my face as he left his father; I had never seen such sadness in a man.

Day after day my master went back to the hilltop where he had waved goodbye to his son. After his time alone praying, he would come back to his tent to rest. The grief and sorrow had really aged the man. His older son tended the flocks and looked after his father's business affairs. After the long day's work, the older son would join his father in his tent for a simple meal and some conversation about the day and turn into bed. These men repeated this routine day after day, week after week, month after month until that day.

That day began like any other breakfast for the master and his older son. There was some small talk before the son went to tend the flocks and the father went to the hilltop to pray. Today the master had walked up the rocky path a little slower than usual. Heartbroken, he raised his arms to pray. I watched from a distance as I went about my chores, when suddenly I saw my master gather his garments and begin to run. Men of his age did not run; it was not dignified. He ran like a shepherd saving a sheep from danger. My heart raced as I thought of what might have caused him to dash down the hill toward the road. Had he seen a poisonous snake? Was there a traveler hurt in the road? His feet were swift and steady as he ran down the rocky path. I ran too, but not as steadily, to his vantage point on top of the hill. Once I reached the summit, I saw the master hugging a skinny younger man.

Both men made their way up the hill. The younger man was dressed in rags, had no shoes, and was covered in dirt and filth. The master had tears running down his face as he approached and had his arms around this smelly shell of a man. Who was this man? The closer they got, he started to look familiar. Was he the long-lost son?

"Bring quickly the best robe, and put it on him, and put a ring on his hand, and shoes on his feet. And bring the fattened calf and kill it, and let us eat and celebrate (Luke 15:22–24 ESV)," the master yelled.

We servants scurried in every direction to meet these commands. The robe woven of fine wool was the clearest blue, with gold trim and tassels; it was even better than the one my master wore. The signet ring was solid gold with the family crest. Only the master and his sons wore these. Sandals of soft brown leather were placed on the young man's feet. The master's son had returned! The joy that the master felt flowed into us all as we prepared the greatest feast ever to be celebrated. The master did not want to let go of his son; he clung onto him, weeping as the son reluctantly recalled his experiences out in the world.

His son told of the young men who quickly befriended him when he got to the city. He told of the great feasts they had enjoyed. He talked about the beautiful women who did things that Hebrew boys' fantasies are about. He had sold all the gold rings and trinkets after all the coins were gone. The famine had come hard into the pagan land, and there was no food or work. The son had gone from house to house searching for work of any kind; the answer was always the same—no. This led him to the most unclean, foul place known to all Jews—the pig farm. At home he had all the comforts he could ever want, but now because of his own bad decisions, he was longing for a leftover pod from the pig slop. Some days the pigs would miss one and he was able to eat. Other days there was not even a scrap left.

Dirty. Hungry. Smelly. Unclean. Broken. His thoughts brought him back to times that were good—not to the false friends and loose women but to us, his father's servants. We are treated well—clothed in clean robes, fresh water to drink, plenty of food to eat, and a place to lay our heads and sleep at night. We had no fear of harsh treatment, for our master was kind. The son had gathered what was left of his life and journeyed home to his father. He had rehearsed his speech a thousand times over as he took each weary step.

"Father, I have sinned against you and against God. Please make me your hired servant." When the father ran to the son, he had not let him make all his speech. His repentance and seeking forgiveness were enough for the father. The father was more than joyful that the son had seen the error of his ways and returned.

The calf that was being fattened for the next dignitary who came for a visit was prepared in the most exquisite sauce of wine, turmeric, and garlic with potatoes, leeks, and figs. Wine was fetched and bread was baked for the amazing feast. The son bathed and put on clean clothes given to him by the father. The father had the son come and recline next to him as all the men and women from the area came to see what had caused the master to run—everyone had seen him earlier in the day. There was food for everyone who came. The tent that had been a house of sorrow had become a home of joy. The songs that played were delightful, and the ladies danced with swirling veils, casting shadows on the tent walls. I tapped my foot to the music as I stood in the door at the ready to serve my master and his son.

As I left the tent to fetch more bread for the guests, I saw the older son approaching the tent. Oh, how happy he would be to see that his brother was home. Soon he would be there and begin rejoicing. He had spent the day far from the tents, tending the flocks. He did not see his father run or his brother return home. He sent in to the servant who attended him to ask what had happened. His response was not as I'd thought—he was angry and refused to go into the tent to celebrate. He was not joyful at all, even when the father came out and pleaded with him. "Son, you are always with me, and all that is mine is yours. It was fitting to celebrate and be glad, for this your brother was dead, and is alive; he was lost, and is found" (Luke 14:31–32 ESV).

The celebration lasted for days; the older son ignored the party by sleeping in a different tent and going out to tend the flock. He acted as if life were normal. Now he grumbled and complained about his brother. "How could my father be so naive? His son hurt him so deeply. Surely he will want more money to leave again soon." The father pleaded with him daily, asking him to join in his joy and forgive his brother as the father had.

We saw how this hurt our master just as much as the younger brother and prayed that he would change his heart and return to the father too.

After the celebration died down, the younger brother began to serve the father like never before—tending the sheep, plowing the fields, and digging wells. He worked harder than any of the hired servants. The older brother learned to work with the younger, but he never fully trusted him.

As Jesus started to explain His stories, I suddenly realized the time of day and quickly scurried back to my master's home. He told these stories, but I knew they were real, for I had seen it happen with my own eyes.

Based on the parable of the prodigal son from Luke 15 ESV.

CHAPTER 10

. . . .

FIGS AND POMEGRANATES

The Woman Caught in Adultery's Story

Mother died giving birth to my youngest sister. The sadness of death mixed with the joy of new life hung heavy in our home. My father tried to manage the household with his servants, but his heart broke that day and he never truly recovered from that great loss. He loved my mother with a deep, rich love, and part of him also died that day. Three years later, my father would join his beloved in his own passing. My older brother had married, and he, along with his new wife, took care of my brother, sisters, and me. This was of course his duty as the eldest son, but the love that had once filled the house was gone. We were orphans, and I was now little more than servant.

I was only eleven years old when my brother started to arrange a marriage for me. The proper martial agreement would gain him prestige in the village, plus he would no longer be burdened with my care. My sister-in-law knew that I was not yet a woman, and so she pleaded with my brother to let me stay until I was trained in the ways of a woman. For the next three years, she taught me to manage a household, how to cook, how to care for children, and how to please a husband. I was afraid of lying with a man, but as soon as I had received my first cycle of uncleanness and learned how to purify myself, I was betrothed.

My husband-to-be was twice my age, a widower with three children who were not that much younger than me. He was a wealthy Pharisee who owned lots of land with vineyards as well as vast herds of livestock. I was thankful for all my sister-in-law had taught me, but my fear rose each day as I waited for him to come fetch me. As the sun rose the day of my wedding, my fear would be made real. He was coming along, with all the village watching. He brusquely took my hand and led me to the rabbi. I could not tell you what the rabbi said as he tied the cord around our hands—my thoughts were on happier times. I tried to push down the terror of this union and hold back my tears.

As we walked through the crowd to the honeymoon tent, I could not contain the tears any longer, and the salty streams of fear flowed freely. When we entered the tent and were alone, he removed my veil and saw my tear-stained cheeks.

"Oh, please Lord, let him be compassionate," was my silent prayer. He raised his hand, I thought to wipe my tears, but I was knocked backward as the back of his hand firmly hit my cheek. He yelled, "Stop crying. You are an embarrassment to me! Remove all your garments and stand here."

I quickly removed my wedding clothes and stood in the middle of the tent. I was afraid to not follow his commands. I tried to cover my womanhood, but he slapped my arms and said I needed to let him see all that he got in this trade. "Trade?" I was once no more than a slave to my brother, and now I would be to this man, my husband.

I could feel his hot breath bearing down on me as he circled my naked body. He removed his clothes and pushed me down onto the wedding bed. Nothing about this day would be beautiful. The fear must have taken over because I do not remember anything until he was fully clothed standing over me, telling me to cleanse myself and join him outside.

He said, "Do not cry like a little girl. I've made you a woman today. Your sister-in-law trained you well, but I will teach you much more."

I bathed my sore, beaten body, put on my wedding dress, and joined him outside the tent. Maybe I was a woman, because as I took his hand, I held my head high and smiled as we went through the crowd. I thought I would be embarrassed, but I felt no shame that day.

I tried to please my husband in all areas of my wifely responsibilities—this saved my face from the back of his hand. He was a hard man to please, and he beat me regularly. Growing up, I had seen such sweet tenderness between my mother and father, but there would be no tenderness from my husband or his children. I knew the pain of losing a mother, so I tried my best to love and care for them, my new family. I prayed with all my heart to know how to make my husband happy. In return, I longed for a kind word, a gentle touch. I thought perhaps that having a child would soften his heart—that would make him love me. But month after month, I did not conceive. The Lord answered me, telling me to wait, and so I waited with all hope. Then it happened; I was pregnant! No amount of bitterness and hate directed at me would steal this joy. I told my husband I was going to bear him a child. I had hoped for elation, but instead I got a beating, the worst I had ever received. I was barely alive as I crawled to wash my wounds and felt the life pass from my womb. I was devastated. With all hope gone, I thought I would rather die than to go on enduring this pain. I went to the temple to pray and implored God to take me from this world, to let me die next time he raised a hand to me.

Each day was filled with a sorrow deeper than the sea. Then one day I was struggling in the marketplace to bring home all my purchases. The streets were overly crowded because of a new rabbi named Jesus. He had many followers, and they all came to our village to hear Him teach in our temple. I bumped into someone, and the figs and pomegranates I had purchased fell from my hands and spilled into the street. I knelt down to scoop up what was not trampled by the crowd, and as I did I saw the man I had bumped into. He had warm, kind, compassionate eyes and was helping me scoop up my fallen fruit. He handed me a pomegranate, and his hand brushed up against my battered arm. There was something healing in his touch. He offered to help me home with my purchases, but I blushed and declined his thoughtful offer. My husband would be furious if I was even seen talking to another man. I gathered everything quickly and scurried home.

I began to put everything away, trying not to daydream about the stranger from the market—about how encouraging his touch would be every day. His voice was warm with kind words, and his deep brown eyes searched into my very soul. I sighed and turned around to see my husband just as he began to beat me. He was calling me names—someone had seen me in the market. I tried to explain what had happened but to no avail. As I lay on the floor, he kicked me one last time and hurled one last insult as he stormed out of the door. He was muttering something about his cheating harlot of a wife and restoring his reputation. There was no talking to him when he was like this. I knew the penalty for cheating, but I was no adulterous woman. I cried myself to sleep right there on the kitchen floor.

I awoke to morning's first light and began to prepare breakfast. I tried to not think about the stranger's kindness or my husband's rage as I called for everyone to come and eat.

My husband had spent the night at the temple with the other Pharisees, and I did not know it at the time, but he had devised a plot to deal with me. After breakfast I began to clean up as my husband told me of his plans to inspect his vineyards and livestock and that he would be gone all day. I asked if he wanted a lunch to take along, but he politely declined. I had a queasy feeling, as he never spoke kindly to me. I decided I would go down to the river to bathe when no one else would be there, so they would not see my bruises, cuts, and scars. Then I would stop in the temple to pray again—surely the Lord would see how bad this was and take my life.

As I was drying off on the shore, I was startled by a noise in the bushes. I quickly put on my garments and headed home. I felt as if there was someone following me. Had my husband hired a spy to make sure I did not talk to any more strangers? As I entered the house, I turned to see who or what had followed me. A man about my age was there.

He whispered, "You are the most beautiful woman I have ever seen. I had to follow you to make sure you were real."

He reached up and brushed the hair away from my face. He leaned in closely and brushed his lips to my neck. My whole body shuddered as I reached to respond to him. All the pain disappeared as he kissed my lips and slid my garment off my shoulder.

Then all the pain flooded back as my husband and the other Pharisees rushed through the door. My husband grabbed my arm and dragged me into the street as I reached for my bathing robe, trying to cover what the stranger had uncovered. My husband and his friends marched me to the temple through the crowded streets. The man followed along, now hurling insults. Adulterous harlot! Fornicator!

They took me to the new rabbi, Jesus, and threw me on the ground before him. I curled my body up, trying to gather my robe around me conceal my nakedness. They said to Him, "Teacher, this woman has been caught in the act of adultery. Now in the Law, Moses commanded us to stone such women. So what do you say?" (John 8:4–5ESV).

Jesus did not look up or join in their insults. He appeared to be calmly writing in the dirt. Then He said, "Let him who is without sin among you be the first to throw a stone at her" (John 8:7 ESV).

One by one by the Pharisees and mob dispersed. As soon as all of them were gone, Jesus asked me where my accusers were. I told Him they were all gone and said that He did not condemn me either. It was then that I realized it was Him, the man I had met yesterday who helped me pick up spilled food. Funny, I was no longer embarrassed and felt none of the shame of being in my bathing robe in the temple when He spoke to me.

His final words were, "Neither do I condemn you; go, and from now on sin no more" (John 8:11 ESV).

One of the women who followed Him covered me with a coat and led me to a safe place among His followers.

This day, through my shame and desperation, I found the most love, understanding and forgiveness through Jesus. I would follow Him from that day on, as He became my heart, my life, The way.

Based on John 8 ESV.

CHAPTER 11

. . . .

TEARS

Martha's Story

I remember the first time Jesus came to our home in Bethany. We heard He was coming, and I began to rush around to get everything in my home perfect for His arrival. We needed to prepare food, fetch extra water for cleaning and drinking, and clean the house from top to bottom. At first my sister helped, but as soon as Jesus and His disciples arrived, she sat down at His feet. The Lord Jesus had chastised me in the most loving and gentle way. I can still hear Him say, "Martha, Martha ..."

I also remember when Mary went to Jerusalem to see Jesus and washed His feet with her tears and nard. She has a special bond with Jesus that I cannot explain. She was willing to give all she had to Him. I was a little more cautious, timid really. I loved Jesus with all my heart, but in our time of need, He didn't come. I was angry! He was only two miles away when our dear brother Lazarus became ill. Two miles! We sent word to Jesus about Lazarus. He loved Lazarus!

That was the most horrible day. Jesus didn't come. My thoughts were filled with sadness, anger, and doubt. Sadness because my brother, my protector, my friend was dead. We put him in the tomb. Jesus didn't come or even send word. Anger turned at Him for pretending to care about us. I doubted what He had taught. He must have been a liar! My emotions came in waves like a storm on the sea.

Laying Lazarus in the tomb was the beginning of our mourning. For seven days, we would sit in the house; other mourners from the town would come and sit with us to console. Women had come and covered our looking glass with fabric, for this was no time to fret over appearances. They came bearing foods of all kinds because we would not be working during our mourning period. On the fourth day Lazarus lay in the tomb—cold, stiff with death, and decay setting in. Jesus finally made His way to our home.

My anger pulsed through me as I took each step to meet Jesus in the road. I wanted to beat Him with my fists, but before I reached Him, I yelled, "Why didn't you come? My brother would have lived if you would have gotten here sooner!"

Jesus came to me, gently pulling me into an embrace. As I cried, my anger was washed away with my tears. He wiped my tears and said, "Don't you know that your brother will rise again?"

Yes, I had heard his teaching, and I believed that in the last days we, His followers, those who believed Him to be the Christ, would rise again on the last day. The trumpet would blow and the dead

WHO DO YOU SAY THAT I AM?

in Christ would rise. This was of no comfort to me. I pleaded with the Lord that if He would have just asked, Lazarus would have been healed. Jesus reminded me that He was the Resurrection and the Life. He asked me to fetch my sister, Mary. I quickly went to the house. I quietly told Mary that Jesus was asking for her. We left the house and walked toward the tomb. All the Jews who had come to mourn with us got up and followed along.

At seeing Jesus, Mary fell at His feet, weeping and pleading for Lazarus's life. My sister felt things at a deeper level than I. He spoke to her and comforted her and asked to go to the tomb. All of us continued on to the place where we had laid Lazarus.

Jesus reached the tomb and began to weep. Maybe there was nothing He could do now. It had been four days. I had wept bitter tears when we had closed the door with the giant stone. Jesus asked that it be moved. Surely He would know the foul, rotting death smell that would be present. I doubt if anyone, even the Lord, would have gone in because the smell of death that now wafted pungently through the whole garden.

Jesus wiped His tears, stepped back from the tomb, and said in a mighty voice, "Lazarus, come forth."

I was standing behind Jesus when I saw a movement inside the tomb. I blinked my eyes rapidly to make sure they were focused and I wasn't seeing things through my tears. Then from the entrance Lazarus came. Our brother was alive!

He was bound at the feet and hands with linen, as was the custom. His head was still wrapped in the towel I had placed there with spices.

65

Mary got to him first and began to unwrap him. She held on to him, crying tears of joy. My tears changed to that of joy too. I went to him and began to inspect him for signs and smells of death. As the linen strips were removed, I could tell he had no signs of decay. He smelled like our brother, not a rotting corpse. He didn't stumble, limp, or seem to be touched at all by sickness or death. He was whole.

For God's glory, Jesus had raised Lazarus from the dead. Our sorrow changed to rejoicing. The walk to the tomb was painful and sad. Walking home, I don't know if my feet were even on the ground. I floated on air as I raced ahead to prepare a few things before Jesus got to our home. The curtains needed to be tied back, the looking glass uncovered, and a banquet table set. The food that was meant for a house of sorrow became food for a banquet. God be praised! Jesus was the real Messiah. That afternoon we sat around the banquet table and talked about the amazing power of God. This day I sat there and listened to every word. I remember the first time Jesus had chastised me, telling me that knowing Him and His teaching were more important than any tasks. I was no longer consumed with trying to please Jesus with my clean house and impeccable cooking. I needed Jesus and Him only.

Based on John 11 ESV.

CHAPTER 12

. . . .

THE FINER THINGS

The Story of Jesus's Anointing

Pharisees live in the nice part of town near the temple. My house was the biggest and nicest house on the street. We had plenty of room for our sons and their spouses, with adjacent quarters for our servants. The room I like best was our great room. My great room lived up to its name. It was as long as it was wide, with windows covered in the finest draperies made. The purple linen would blow with the breeze, creating dancing shadows in every corner of the room while making patterns on the table. I hadn't seen a table like mine anywhere, not even at the high priest's home. To say it was gorgeous wasn't enough; it was perfection. The best carpenter in all of Israel had made my table—the legs were ornately carved to look like to paws of a great lion, and the top was a solid piece of acacia wood (not planks like lesser tables) that had been sanded and polished until I could see myself in the glossy finish. The table was surrounded with the best cushions money could buy. Linen of every deep, rich color was stuffed with feathers until the seams were barely able to close.

If my walls could talk, they would tell you of all the dinners with famous guests who had been there in my great room. My husband was a Pharisee from the tribe of Levi and Pharisee among the Pharisees. He went to the temple every day to teach the younger men and see to the political affairs of Israel. Many nights the conversations for the temple continued in our home over dinner. My servants and I were always on the ready for whoever came home for dinner. Talk as of late had been of this man named Jesus and His twelve followers. I didn't know much about politics, but I had heard enough to know He was a threat to our Jewish way of life. He was some kind of madman who said He was sent from God. A blasphemer is what He was. He was from Nazareth, and we all knew nothing good ever came out of Nazareth.

As I was telling the servants to get the table and washing station ready, He walked in my door. My husband had brought that madman and his followers into my pristine home. I knew it would take weeks to get the stench of Nazareth out of my cushions. For honored guests, I would motion for the servants to wash the days walking dust off of their feet. Today I stood with my arms crossed in anger and told no one to wash even a toe! My house was defiled! I would no longer be the envy of the ladies. I would be the laughingstock.

My life as I knew it was over. I was put to shame in my own home. As I was stalking across the room to have a word with my husband, I picked up the pitcher of wine. I leaned over to pour some in his cup and was about to whisper my comments of displeasure on how this evening was unfolding when she came in uninvited. No one of my standing would know this woman. I could tell just by looking at her what she was—a harlot. Her threadbare dress hugged all her womanly curves. Her head was uncovered so you could see her flowing jet-black hair and crimson painted-on lips in sharp contrast to her pale skin that rarely saw the light of day. She was a woman of the night.

She entered my house unannounced, unwelcome, uninvited, and knelt at Jesus's feet. She had in her hands a beautiful perfume jar. I had jars like this in my room full of spices and oils to adorn myself, but how did she have one? These were the costliest alabaster jars. In the heat I had often cooled my face on the smooth sides of white pure alabaster. She opened the jar, and the smell of pure frankincense and nard filled the room, overpowering the stench of sweaty Nazarenes. I knew these scents. The memories of using them for burial rites and during the days of grief flooded my soul. How could such a woman afford something so beautiful and costly?

The woman was weeping. As she knelt at Jesus's feet, her fat, salty tears wet his feet, and she dried them with her flowing hair. She then poured the anointing oil on His feet and began to kiss them over and over. My husband spoke up, saying, "If this man is truly a prophet, He would have known who and what this woman touching Him was, for she is a sinner."

I thought this would stir up the controversy, but instead Jesus answered by telling a story about a money collector! A madman, harlot, and now stories of money collectors. What did these three people have in common other than being the lowest of the low among the Jews? I got lost in the story and began to notice the crowd forming outside of my house. The shame I felt was great, and I hurriedly scurried to close my beautiful purple drapes. Had I gotten there in time to close out the pitiful judgmental stares, or would my shame be spread throughout the entire city like the wind carrying a stray feather?

Jesus' story ended by asking if the person with the big debt or small was forgiven more. The big debtor is what my husband answered. Remember, my husband was a Pharisee, so his answers on these matters had to be right. He was trained in the laws. Next Jesus began to scold my husband for not washing His feet, greeting Him with a kiss, or anointing His head with oil. Even a madman would know that these common acts were for friends and invited guests, not crazy blasphemers. Jesus's next statement stopped me in my tracks. A cold chill ran down my spine as He said her sins were forgiven by her faith. Faith! She was a harlot! How did she have faith in the one true God of Israel? Prostitutes were not allowed in the temple. Jesus said her sins were forgiven? How did He know that? He couldn't forgive sins. Only the priest could forgive sins on the Day of Atonement when the proper sacrifice was made. It was not the Day of Anointment! He was not a priest! There had been no sacrifices made! A harlot forgiven by a madman!

The room suddenly became black. Next thing I remember is waking up in my room with my servants fanning me with long palm furans. As I sat up, my head ached as memories surfaced of the madman and harlot. Had this been all a dream? I hoped with all hope it was only a dream and I wasn't going to live with the shame. Oh, the great shame of the day the madman and His harlot entered my house.

The above story is based on Luke 7:36–50 ESV.

CHAPTER 13

PITCHERS AND TOWELS

Story of a Follower

I am no one of significant standing, just a woman who once followed John the Baptist. We all knew that he was not The One. He was preparing the way for Him, the Messiah, the King, and our hope.

One day, Jesus came with His followers to where John was baptizing. As Jesus approached the water, a reverent hush fell over the crowd that just minutes ago had been loud from all the conversations. As He set foot in the water, there was an eerie silence; it would seem that even all of nature was silent for what was about to happen.

John said," Behold, the Lamb of God, who takes away the sin of the world!" (John 1:29 ESV). John said he was not worthy to untie this man's sandals. What? He did not look like a king. A king is regal. This man looked normal. He had only fishermen and everyday men following Him. Even a tax collector was among them. We all know what kind of sinners they are. Where were His mighty warriors? John and his men in their rugged camelhair robes looked more like the king's mighty men than Jesus and His men.

Jesus made His way through the crowd down the banks of the river and stepped into to cool water. As John lowered Him into the water, an earth- shaking voice came from heaven, "This is My Son, with Whom I am well pleased" (Matthew 3:17 ESV). A dove then came from out of the clouds and rested on Jesus as He came out of the water. Light usually comes from the sky to the earth, but not today. A radiant, blinding aura surrounded Jesus. These rays weren't shining down on Him. Beams were coming out of Him. Following John, I had seen hundreds of people baptized, but I had never experienced anything that compared even close to this.

Could Jesus be the King? Our hope? Our Savior? I had been following John; my loyalty belonged to him. Serving him was such an honor. How could my heart be changed so fast? Had I become a fickle woman, changing my mind every time I saw someone more desirable, more prominent? No, John had predicted that the Christ was coming, and I needed to follow Jesus. I said my goodbyes, quickly packed my belongings, and followed Jesus.

There were other women following Him too. He was so kind. And the miracles He did were beyond amazing. The Pharisees and other leaders began accusing Him of doing His miracles in the name of Beelzebub and worse yet, of blasphemy. How could this be? Were they seeing what I was seeing?

As their rumblings grew louder, Jesus became more private. He pulled those who followed Him closely in around Him. Following

Him were the twelve disciples, a handful of additional men, and the faithful women. I was honored to serve with the faithful women.

Well, enough about me. Let me tell you about what I would later know as Jesus's last Passover.

Jesus followed the customs of the Jews and celebrated all the feasts. Passover this time was different from the beginning. He had sent us ahead of Him to Jerusalem, as usual. You see, there were many things that had to be done to celebrate properly. The disciples found a room above a house that was not going to be used. Finding a house during the feasts was always difficult, and you had to take what you could get. I thought we would have a lot to do once we got there, but this upper room was perfect. The main room was large, with a beautiful soft rug, a large table, and many big, fluffy cushions, and it was clean.

When we arrived, the ladies began the ritual cleaning. All the leaven had to be removed from the house. We opened all the shutters and began removing the cushions and rug. We took these outside to be shaken and beaten to make sure that not even a crumb too small for a mouse was left. While some were outside, we began wiping down the counters, tables, and windowsills, and even the walls. Then the sweeping and resweeping began. We used big brooms and small whisks to remove every speck of leaven. If any was found, it had to be burned. I heard of some women selling their leaven to their pagan neighbors and buying it back on the eighth day. This practice was dishonest, so we burned the crumbs we found in our rented upper room. After the room was clean, we prepared the pots, pans, plates, cups, and implements of serving.

As we cleaned, the disciples went to acquire all that we needed. They purchased a spotless, perfect lamb. Wine, bitter herbs, the ingredients for unleavened bread and charoset, potatoes, and salt were also purchased. The upper room was a buzz of activity: cooking, washing, and fetching water and things from the market. I was making charoset, chopping apples and nuts to mix with honey and wine. Each of the dishes to be prepared had symbolic meaning. The perfect lamb was to be sacrificed for our sin offerings. The bitter herbs were to remind us of the removed, bitter, harsh treatment the fathers received as slaves in Egypt. The charoset, which I make the best, was to remind us of the mortar that they used to build the Great Pyramids. The potatoes were boiled, and we dipped them in saltwater to remind us of all the tears shed in Egypt. The matzoth was to remind us of how fast God moved them from Egypt; there was no time to let the bread rise.

Two days before the Passover meal, we stopped our preparations to have supper with the Rabbi. Here is where it becomes out of the ordinary.

Before we began serving, He got up took a pitcher, basin, and towels for the ritual foot washing. We had spent all afternoon washing the large, perfect pottery pitcher and the pristine basin in preparation for the Passover. He removed His outer garment, unfolded the towel, and tied it at His waist like a servant. He was two days early. Why was He using the special implements? Why was He lowering Himself to wash feet?

Peter is always vocal, but when Jesus began washing their feet, Peter went completely mad. His anger burned; he wanted no part of the foot washing. I understood. I felt like I needed to be serving the Rabbi, not Him serving me. But then Jesus said that if Peter refused to have his feet washed, he was refusing Jesus. Peter's attitude change was so quick it left my head swimming. He now wanted Jesus to wash every part of him. Jesus said something very puzzling next: "The one who has bathed does not need to wash, except for his feet, but is completely clean. And you are clean, but not every one of you" (John 13:10 ESV). Who needed to bathe? They had all come to the upper room clean and ready for the Passover.

I loved listening to the words of Jesus, but tonight they were very troubling to my heart. He spoke of the one who would betray Him, Peter denying Jesus, His going away, yet not abandoning us. I did not know how all these things would be true, but I know that Jesus had always been honest. My heart was troubled and could not imagine what I would do if Jesus left. How could He leave without abandoning us?

As the dinner wrapped up, we were all somber. None of us wanted to leave Him, so we followed Him to the garden where He often prayed. The garden was filled with flowering plants that gave off a sweet aroma in the night air. He wanted to be alone, so He asked us to stay and pray at the entrance of the garden. We settled in to pray on the lush green grass. Jesus took eleven disciples with Him deeper into the garden. Someone said they saw Judas leave before Jesus blessed the wine and the bread. No one seemed concerned about where he had gone. I assumed he had to take care of some more details for the Passover meal. I heard that once inside, Jesus just took John, James, and Peter farther with Him. He asked them to watch and pray. All of us eventually went to sleep on the lush grass with blankets of sweet aromas. You know it's hard to stay awake after a hard day's work followed by a good meal

As I prayed and tried to be comforted, I kept going back to what Jesus had said.

"Peace I leave with you; my peace I give to you. Not as the world gives do I give to you. Let not your hearts be troubled, neither let them be afraid. You heard me say to you, 'I am going away, and I will come to you.' If you loved me, you would have rejoiced, because I am going to the Father, for the Father is greater than I. And now I have told you before it takes place, so that when it does take place you may believe. I will no longer talk much with you, for the ruler of this world is coming. He has no claim on me, but I do as the Father has commanded me, so that the world may know that I love the Father" (John 14:27–31 ESV).

Many more things happened the next forty-eight hours that changed not just my life, but also the entire world.

Based on Jesus's baptism, Matthew 3, and the night of His arrest in John 13:1:35, John 14 ESV.

. . . .

CHAPTER 14

THE NIGHT MY HUSBAND DID NOT COME HOME

The Story of Peter's Denial

Passover season is usually such a joyful occasion with the family gathering and the flurry of activities of preparation. Telling stories of our amazing exodus from Egypt to the children always brings me such a warm and happy feeling. I remember my great-grandparents telling the same stories but with their own life experiences. My cousins and I were so competitive when trying to find afikoman. The afikoman is the middle piece of matzo that is broken in the early part of the Seder meal to represent the two temples. The half that is removed from the table is wrapped in a napkin and hidden. My uncles took turns hiding afikoman until my cousins were men and it was their turn. There were such squeals and giggling if you were the winner. The winner, who demanded a ransom for finding the dessert matzo, had bragging rights for the entire year. The prize for finding it was a wonderful date and nut candy dripping in honey that my great-grandmother made. We all got some of this sweet confection, but the first bite was such a privilege. My mouth waters just thinking of this honey nut treat. The recipe has been passed down to everyone and is still part of our celebration. The stories from the Haggadah are familiar, but every year I am reminded of the ten plagues and the quick exodus. God has been very good to my people; this was so evident as my grandfathers, uncles, and father read the stories. Some of you may be asking: Weren't you supposed to be somber and reverent? Yes, there was a holy reverence to this night, but there was so much joy throughout all of Jerusalem. The hand of God from oppressive slavery had delivered the Israelites; for that we celebrate.

This year there was a strange ice-cold breeze in the air. The Jewish leaders all seemed so upset. Everywhere I went getting my preparations in order, there were rumblings and rumors about this man. His name was Jesus. Some said He was going around healing people and doing other signs; some thought Satan must have been possessing Him. He was claiming to be the Son of God, our Messiah and King. If you had seen the band of men who followed Him, you would have doubted His royal line. They were fishermen, a tax collector, a doctor, and some other professions. But their professions did not matter. None of these men worked in their professions anymore. They gave up all they had and followed Jesus. They only had the clothes on their backs, ate what was given to them or that was bought with money given to them, and slept wherever people would allow them. Kings' men lived in tents or quarters within the palace. They were clothed in uniforms and had more than one, and the food these men ate was a feast every day. There was no way this man was the long-expected king. I knew more law than most women because I was from the tribe of Levi. My parents had arranged my marriage from a young age to a man, Jacob, from that tribe as well. Jacob served in the temple, and he taught me many great things about our heritage. I was proud to be a Jew from the tribe of Levi. There is such prestige, even as a woman.

The rumblings within Jerusalem began to concern me two nights before the Passover. My husband was not home to provide the usual comfort for my fears this night. After the kids were tucked in and fast asleep, I slipped on my outer garment and out into the cold dark in search of my husband. My Jacob would have answers for all these rumors. He would calm my fears and worries, and I would soon return home for a great night's sleep. As I walked toward Caiaphas's home that evening, there were many more people out than should have been. Caiaphas was the high priest and as such was the overseer of my husband's job. I assumed that if Jacob were anywhere, he would be there. Caiaphas would have answers. I walked with purpose, but with each step I heard more rumors and talk of killing Jesus.

I got to the house as, I saw the armed men take Him into the priestly chambers. I had been inside a few times. The room they took him to was long and narrow. It was not much to look at. I thought that it was actually a very cold place—the kind of place that chills your soul. The room was for trials and bringing grievances to the High Priest. I would not be allowed into that room tonight while this late-night trial was happening. Women weren't allowed to enter the room while business was happening. I had not been there for that purpose but had passed through a couple of times during a celebration. Just thinking of the room made me shiver, so I got closer to the fire to warm up before continuing my search for Jacob.

The amount of people there made it hard to get close. How had all these people gotten past the guards at the gate? They knew me. I was Jacob's wife. I had not seen most of them, and I am good with faces. Most of the faces tonight looked angry. These faces made me uneasy, and the fear that had driven me to find Jacob was prominent again. I would need to find Jacob, but I was cold, so I stayed by the charcoal fire.

As I stood there trying to become warm, I scanned the people, hoping that someone would look peaceful or familiar. There was one man I knew I had not seen before. He looked like those followers of Jesus. He was burly and unkempt. Just as I summoned the courage to ask who he was, a young servant girl came and asked what I know we must have all been thinking.

"You also are not one of this man's disciples, are you?" (John18:17 ESV), she asked.

He replied that he was not. But there was something in his "not" that seemed like a yes. Others must have noticed that he did not belong here. A man came up right, as these words were about to come out of my mouth. He asked if this man was a follower. Again there was something not truthful in his denial. No sooner had his denial been uttered than Malcus's brother, a servant to the high priest asked again. This time he had seen this man in the olive grove that night. I think you would remember what the man who cut off your brother's ear looked like. Again he denied it. As he denied it, a rooster began to crow. I so was engrossed with the story of the cut-off ear that I did not see the man slip off into the dawning light. This guy by the fire had cut off Malcus's ear, but Jesus had picked it up off of the ground and put it back on his head. Must have been some more tricks by this man and this Jesus. The rooster had crowed. Dawn was breaking. I rushed home to tend to our children. They would be rising soon. I would not have time to even lay my head down at all. I had not seen Jacob, but I knew from the rumblings he might be there for a while. It was a long day.

Based on Peter's denial told in John 18:15–18 ESV.

. . . .

CHAPTER 15

WASHBASINS

Pontius Pilate's Story

Roman women like me are far prettier than any Jewish woman. My skin is flawless, hair the perfect shade of raven black with curly waves throughout, and my lips red and full like the pomegranate, and my body curves in all the right places. My wardrobe was full of tasteful gowns that hugged my body just so and scarves and jewels to add the perfect addition to every outfit. I looked good on the arm of my husband, as any politician's wife should. We married when he was studying the laws in Rome. His fellow students had nicknamed him Pontius Pilate—Pilate means the one who grows hair. He hated his hairy moniker and told everyone it really meant plunderer, but my husband was too fair and kind to raid and steal.

After his studies were complete, we moved to of all places Jerusalem in Israel. No one wanted to be assigned to this lowly place, but hopefully his great skill would move us up the political ladder quickly. He would be governor of this remote region and of the Jews—not Roman citizens. Ruling the Jews was typically easy. They followed such strict religious laws that addressed all areas of life. Their leaders even said to give to Caesar what was Caesar's, so they paid all the taxes. The only time there was any trouble was when they had their festivals. There was this one when they asked the Romans to release a prisoner and save him from execution. I did not understand why we had to let a criminal out, but every year Pontius brought out two men, and the crowd would choose who would be released.

The crowd would begin lowly murmuring among themselves until there was a frenzied outcry. Pontius would step out onto the balcony, and a hush would fall over the crowd. He looked so regal in his robes and laurel crown. I would stand behind him in my best robes and marvel at his power. The guards would come out on the liana, escorting the most dreadful men. Battered and bruised, not able to hold themselves at attention, the prisoners would be presented.

"Kneel before your lord, the governor!" the captain of the guard would yell.

Some men would curse and spit, refusing to pay homage to my husband. This was upsetting to me, but with a raise of one my husband's fingers, the guards would strike the ruffian and make him kneel. He wielded such power, but he was so fair and compassionate. I never saw the powerful side personally. I only saw his love.

Many other politicians' wives felt used—they were to be pretty, quiet, and subservient. Pontius loved me, and I loved him. He told me how valuable I was to him with my beauty, poise, and hospitality and as his friend most of all. Every night when he came home from his busy day handing down rulings and making laws, I would make sure that dinner would be ready. With a clap of my hands, the table would be laid out with dishes of lamb, couscous, dates, olives, figs, and juicy pomegranates. I made sure that the lamb was seasoned with the right amount of saffron, the couscous cooked to perfection, the olives at peak ripeness, and the fruit picked at their sweetest. Wine, olive oil, and honey were in pitchers at the ready to pour. I would make sure I was clean and perfumed when he returned home. Pilate would lack for nothing. I attended his every need, but most of all, I was a safe place for him to unload the worries of the day. As he ate, I would massage his shoulders, and he would tell me the problems of the day.

I would try to distract his worries by telling him stories I had heard in the market and about my day. His favorite was when I would tell him about my dreams. Our gods had given me the gift of dreams so I could tell the future. Well, most of the time I was right. My vivid dreams were an encouragement to my husband and helped him make some hard decisions.

After dinner we would light incense before we offered sacrifices to Jupiter, Neptune, Juno, Mars, and Venus. I would plead in my prayers to Venus for dreams to help my husband make wise rulings. Breathing deeply the scents of frankincense, sandalwood, and myrrh mixed with burning grains filled my lungs and brought me to the heavens and close to the gods. As we finished our worship, we would walk down the long hallway filled with statues of our gods that led to our bedchambers and turn in for the night.

Servants were there to help us remove the heavy day robes and prepare for sleep. My bed was as soft as a cloud, filled with many small pillows, and draped in the finest silk linens. Each night I would cuddle up with the pillows surrounding me—lost in the pillows and blankets, I would soon be lost in my amazing dreams. At the ready beside me was a scribe to write down my dreams as soon as I awoke—day or night.

For weeks I had heard about one of their rabbis, Jesus. They said He was going to overthrow the government. This made me worry at first, and then I recalled the power and might of the Roman army. Caesar was our king, and no Jew would ever take his place. The Jews could not be their own rulers. We had conquered them, and now they needed us to rule over them. But still there was a strange feeling in my soul.

"Venus, give me rest and show me dreams to help my husband with this Jew," I prayed.

I drifted off to sleep, confident that Venus would grant my request. Sleep came to me fast—dreamland was not in vivid color tonight. Muted gray faces of two men drifted in front of the palace. One face was disfigured and angry, and the other exuded a silent peace. Suddenly the grotesque face was on the balcony with my husband, whispering in his ear. My husband was in muted color too, as if he weren't fully alive. Then I saw his hands red with blood. The peaceful man was Jesus, and Pilate needed to have nothing to do with Him. I awoke in a cold sweat and pulled my robe about me as I ran into his adjoining bedchamber. Bursting through the door, I began to tell of the faces in my dream.

"Have nothing to do with Jesus!" I exclaimed. "Wash your bloody hands of Him!"

Pontius sat up in bed and bid me to come to him. I was shaking in fear. Something bad was going to happen because of Jesus—something bad to my husband. He gently took my hands and explained that there was no need for worry; Jesus had not been arrested. Further, Jesus was a Jew, and they dealt with their own. He would not have to pass any rulings over Jesus. Holding me in his arms had helped remove some of my worries, but my dream haunted me all day. It was almost time for their festival where one criminal would be pardoned and set free. I went about my daily duties and had prepared myself in my most regal gown, the purple one that Pontius liked on me best, for his return that evening. He was usually home when the sun was sinking in the west, making the Jerusalem sky bright orange with streaks of pink. Tonight the sun was lower in the sky that was turning indigo. The servants lit the torches and candles throughout the palace. The warm yellow lights would welcome him home soon. As the shadows danced on the walls, I waited and worried. He sent word to me that he would not be home for dinner. I would take dinner to him and had the servants help me pack a large willow basket with his favorites, and I dashed to the part of the palace where he worked.

I stopped cold in my track as I rounded the corner to enter the courtyard. It was the face in my dream. Jesus was the face. Though He was beaten and bruised, He had the most peaceful countenance. Looking in His deep brown eyes, I saw such compassion and love. What was His crime? Surely this man was innocent.

"He's a blasphemer!" said the man next to my husband. Blasphemy was a Jewish crime.

Wash your hands of all of them, was the thought that I just could not get to leave my mouth. Try as I might, my throat was dry and took my words. My husband sent Him away. Jesus would need to be tried in the Jewish courts. Good riddance! I knew nothing good was going to come of this proceeding.

I rushed to his side with a basin of water, "Here, wash your hands, and be rid of Jesus," I said as the men escorted Him to Caiaphas their high priest's home.

We walked back to our private quarters in the palace and decided just to turn in. The day had taken all of Pontius' strength. I made sure that his servants were at the ready to serve him before I kissed him good night. I took a walk in the cool, night air of my gardens. The smell of gardenias filled the air as I paced and prayed. Restless, I lay in my luxurious bed, hoping that the two faces would not torment my sleep tonight. I had never prayed for no dreams, but I did tonight.

Late in the night I was startled awake by the noise of a mob. The Jews were back with Jesus! Now Pontius would have to deal with them all! I quickly dressed and rushed to stand behind him in my rightful place. He would try to be fair, as he knew that Jesus had committed no Roman crime. As soon as daylight kissed the sky, the crowd demanded that Barabbas be released.

As soon as the sentence of crucifixion was pronounced, Pontius called for a golden basin. He publically washed his hands before we turned into the palace together. Both of us walked with our heads held high until we reached our private chamber and the servants dismissed.

"What have I done, wife? This man is innocent," he said as he began to weep.

Based on John 18 ESV.

CHAPTER 16

GRIEF THAT WAS AND WAS NOT

Mary's Story

Sadness hung in the air of the upper room like the stale air of a long winter. Our Jesus had died. I wept until I had no more tears. Then I cried more without the aid of tears to cool my red, hot, swollen eyes and cheeks. There are seven stages of grief one must go through, and I went through all of them several times that first day. My emotions came in waves over a stormy sea. How could any of us go on? The Rabbi was dead. Life no longer had meaning, and I felt as though I was falling down the steepest cliff headed to the bottom. The sharp, pointy rocks of death would be better than reliving His death over and over. I had lived for Him, and now He was dead.

No one wanted to celebrate Passover this year. None of us felt like worshiping our God. He had taken Jesus from us. The faithful who were left persuaded us all to do what was right. With no emotion left, in complete exhaustion, I was obedient to the law, and I did what had to be done. Through my tears and inconsolable sadness, I observed the Passover.

As I looked back over the last two days, I wondered, why had they crucified Him? Jesus had done nothing wrong. His crucifixion had been so horrific. The Roman guards had used rods and whip to beat Him beyond recognition. John had gone with Him to Caiaphas's home, where the trials and beating began. Caiaphas was the high priest. His house was near the temple. For most occasions, it was a place of celebration. Being the high priest afforded him the right to such a large, palatial home with several long rooms for feasts and banquets. But there was no music wafting out of the windows today— only the mocking and jeering of the crowd and the horrible blows they laid on Jesus's back.

John had gone with Jesus. Maybe John's influence could make them stop. John loved Jesus so much. I do not know how he could stand by and watch. John was much stronger than me. With every blow and crack of the whip, I would have screamed as if they were torturing me.

I could hardly look at Him on the way to Calvary. His face was bloody and twisted. The dirt from the road and the night fires mingled with the blood that flowed down from the crude thorn crown they had pushed into His skull. His back was open, raw, red, and bloody. The weight of the cross pushed Him down with every step. As He moved, the rough cross dug deeper into His raw flesh. He was stripped of everything that made Him look human. He never screamed or cried out for God to save Him. His eyes were focused and determined as

He took each excruciating step toward His death. I could not handle looking at Him any longer. I felt His pain with Him. I slipped away from John and Mary. I had seen enough, and I was physically ill.

The crowd hurled insults, spit on Him, and pushed Him down. The soldiers did not stop them. They encouraged the crowd and joined in. The crowd that condemned Him watched as the Romans crucified Jesus and two other men. The other men were criminals and acted like it—hurling insults back at the crowd, spitting on the guards. One of them mocked Jesus while he himself hung next to Him. Jesus hung there like a common thief and murderer. He hung by large nails that were driven into each arm at the wrist. His legs were spiked together at the ankles. The other men fought and tried to get away from the guards. Jesus lay down on the rough wood and made no attempts to escape.

Did not these guards see that He was not like the others? Could not they see the kindness in His eyes? I looked past His mangled body to look into His kind, loving eyes once more. What had they done to Him? There was no more kindness in His eyes, only pain and sorrow. I had to catch my breath. I was woozy from all I was seeing. This was the worst grief I had every felt. I tried to stay by Mary's side to encourage and pray with her. When they pierced His side, the blood and water flowed freely from His side. He was dead; there was no doubt left. I could take no more. I hugged Mary and slipped into the confusing crowd. Some of the men who had condemned and cursed Him now looked sad and guilty. Some were still mocking Him, and the last few were slipping away with their heads down.

The blood and water flowed from His side. There was no possibility that He survived. Since it was near the time for Sabbath, Joseph of Arimathea and Nicodemus asked Pilate for Jesus's body. These men were wealthy and well thought of in the Jewish community but had secretly followed Jesus. Nicodemus had brought linen strips soaked in myrrh, aloe, and spices. The smell of these strips made me think of death—the death of my grandparents, my father, and my mother. I did not like this smell, and I was not ready for my Jesus to smell of death.

Joseph arranged for a tomb nearby in a flowering garden. The cave was carved out of the side of a hill covered in grapevines and wild flowers. There was a sweet fragrance of summer and new life wafting in the air. These two different smells mingled together, but the smell of death overpowered the smell of life, and I began to weep.

I returned to our rented upper room where the eleven disciples, Mary of Magdalena, Mary of Bethany, Martha, Lazarus, and the other followers had gathered. As the sun began to sink in the western sky, Sabbath was upon us, and nothing else could be done for Jesus. That night we read the Shamot scrolls, and John recited the Haggadah, telling the story of Israel's delivery from slavery. These stories of promised hope lay flat this year. We were now a people of no hope. Jesus was not on the throne in Jerusalem. We were still under the thumb of the Roman soldiers at the bidding of Caesar. This Passover Jesus lay in His tomb, our hope buried alongside Him. Had everything He said been lies? I had no more tears as I tried to sleep. My eyes stung, my face ached, and my head was full of all Jesus had said. Finally my exhaustion took over, and I fell asleep.

The first day of the week arrived like no other—sun coming up in the east, the soft humming of morning prayers. I got up and began to prepare food for breakfast, fetch water, and pack up my things to return home. I did not pray that morning. I could not. Jesus was dead, and I had followed false hope.

We all would need to return home to Nazareth, Cana, Bethlehem, Bethany, and many other small villages. None were ready to return home. We wanted to stay and comfort each other. Mary and the disciples needed us to mourn with them. This Jesus had not lived up to His promises. He said He was going away but was not going to abandon us, but I had never felt so alone. He was gone. Had all He said been a lie? Had I believed a madman? What was it I had really seen in His eyes? Beyond the sorrow, I felt betrayed. I was no longer sad—I was furious and confused.

What happened next shocked me to my core. Mary Magdalene had arisen while it was still dark and walked to the tomb. Her sorrow had driven her there to mourn alone. When she got to the opening of the cave, the heavy stone was rolled away, and the guards were nowhere to be seen. Out of fear for what the people had done with Jesus' body, she ran to find some help. She found John and Peter. John and Peter had never run as fast as they did that morning, racing for the tomb. John got there a little before Peter but froze at the entrance. He was taking it all in—the heavy stone that took four men to roll it in place had been moved, and the soldiers who stood guard had disappeared or run away. Questions swirled about in his head. He was about to go in when Peter charged ahead and went right inside. John joined him, and they found the linen strips neatly folded where His body lay and His headpiece folded where His head would have been. When the disciples returned with the story, the sorrow that I thought had reached its limit grew until I was physically weak.

Mary, however, could not leave the tomb. She stayed in the garden to weep alone. Alone was how she had come to Jesus, and she was alone with her grief. She looked another time and then went into the cave to collect the linen strips. If she did not have Jesus, then she would have these strips to remember Him. She needed something of Him to grasp, to hold. Through the tears, she saw the most beautiful and powerful creatures inside the tomb where Jesus had been. She blinked back the tears and rubbed her eyes. This was no illusion. How had these massive men slipped past her into the tomb? Had they been the ones to move Jesus? They asked her why she was weeping. As she answered the questions about her cries, she could feel someone close behind her.

She turned, thinking it was maybe the gardener. She demanded that he tell where he had taken Jesus. As the man spoke her name, she recognized the voice. Jesus had said her name. Jesus. Had. Said. Her. Name. How could this be? She too had seen Him die on the cross with the water and the blood flowing out of His side. Mary's tears turned from sorrowful to exuberant joy. She held on to Jesus and begged Him to return with her so that the others could experience this great joy too.

He said that it was not time for His return just yet and urged her to return to the disciples. She needed to tell them what she had seen.

Mary ran back to the upper room where the disciples had gathered to discuss where they had taken Him. They also devised a plan for when they would be questioned by the Jews

Mary burst through the door, breathlessly proclaiming that she had seen Jesus. At first we thought she had found where they had taken His body. She assured us that she had seen Him. Jesus was standing up and holding her as she clung to Him, crying.

"He's alive! He's alive!" she kept saying.

Mary had been possessed by seven demons when Jesus healed her. That had been almost three years ago. Had these demons come back to Mary in her sorrow? Had they made her believe that the gardener was Jesus?

The disciples locked up the upper room and prepared for the worst as night began to fall. Would the Jews be coming for us next? They arranged who would stay awake by the door if the guards came. After a small meal that no one really ate, the most amazing thing happened. Jesus was here! He was in our midst! The door was locked, with no way to get inside. But there He was, standing, talking. He was alive! Jesus was here. I wish that Thomas had been here to see this. He was not going to believe this.

Jesus would come to us in many ways over the next few days. The things He taught us began to become clear. Jesus was alive!

The above story was based on John 19–20 ESV.